Lydie and her Second Chance Next Door

A Clean Small Town Romance

K.C. Kirkland

Copyright © 2023 by K.C. Kirkland

All rights reserved.

No part of this book may be reproduced in any form or by any electronic or mechanical means, including information storage and retrieval systems, without written permission from the author, except for the use of brief quotations in a book review.

❀ Created with Vellum

Chapter One

Lydie

I'm a baker, not a public speaker, so only the good Lord knows why I agreed to give a speech to all of the guests present tonight.

Of course, I had to do it – they were there to see me after all.

My niece, Tori, and her husband, Sam, had gone all out in making sure this was a memorable celebration for me, and I could hardly believe what I saw before me.

My bakery had been transformed for the night. The familiar walls were adorned with lilies and orchids, their gentle fragrance filling the air. The tables were dressed in pristine white tablecloths, looking like a scene from a dream.

Caterers bustled around, arranging an array of treats inspired by my own cherished recipes. The sight of my pastries, cakes, and delicacies laid out so beautifully left me feeling humbled and overwhelmed with gratitude. There was champagne, sparkling and bubbling like the laughter of angels, to toast to this momentous occasion.

I couldn't help but feel a profound sense of love and blessedness. It was as if God Himself had bestowed his blessing upon my life's work, and I couldn't have been more thankful.

Looking around at the faces of my family, friends, and loyal customers, I felt a deep connection with each and every one of them. They were the ones who had supported me through the highs and lows, and it was their unwavering faith in me that had led to this magical moment.

But I was still afraid of talking among large groups of people.

Soon, I started to fidget.

I was lost in my own world that I didn't see Tori and Sam approach me. Tori waved her hand in front of my face to get my attention.

"Are you okay, Aunt Lydie?"

"Yes, I think so, just a bit nervous."

"Don't be!" Tori said, cheerfully. "Everyone is here to see you, celebrate you. Just talk as if you're talking to friends...but there just so happens to be a microphone in front of your face."

I can do this. *Just friends, like Tori said.*

Except nothing was ever easy.

Looking down at my notecards for what felt like the twelfth time that night already, I didn't see him walk up to me. I didn't even know he was there until he called my name.

"Lydie?"

Reflexively, I looked up...and immediately lost my balance.

I was staring into the face of a man I hadn't seen in years, a man I still loved.

Jack Weston.

I tried to catch myself as my legs tangled with each other, but unfortunately, when my hand came down to right myself from falling, it landed on a plate with a slice of cake that had heavy amounts of frosting.

Of course, the embarrassment didn't stop there.

Jack noticed I was unbalanced and tried to help. His face came forward just at the same time I lifted my dessert-covered hand and his cheek collided with my palm.

So, not only did it look like I was slapping him, but I left a trail of broken cake across his skin.

"Oh, no, I am so sorry!" I gasped out.

Behind me, I heard my nephew-in-law say to his wife, "You Dawson women really have a way with cake."

Panicked, I grabbed a few napkins from the table and started blotting at his face. I heard him let in a little gasp as I stepped closer to him, my hand against his cheek as I wiped the dessert off of him.

It didn't even cross my mind how intimate it might look until I made the mistake of looking up.

As I gazed into his eyes, time itself seemed to fold, bending and twisting until I was no longer standing in the present. Those steely gray eyes, so familiar and yet foreign after all these years, held me captive.

It was as if the years that had passed since we were last together simply melted away, and I was transported back to that time when we were young and the world was ours to conquer.

. . .

His eyes were a paradox, both intense and gentle, like liquid metal that could mold itself to any emotion he wished to convey. They were a reflection of his soul, a window into a world that I had once been a part of. The depth and complexity in those eyes drew me in, like a moth to a flame, and I found myself momentarily lost in their all-consuming presence.

Looking at him now made it feel as if no time had passed at all.

The lines etched by age seemed to disappear, leaving only the memory of the boy I had fallen in love with. His eyes were the same, unchanged by the passing years, and they held the power to unravel me completely.

I could feel my heart racing, the same way it had when I was eighteen and experiencing love for the first time. The rush of emotions was overwhelming, a storm of nostalgia, longing, and a hint of apprehension.

In all my life, I had never seen eyes like his—eyes that held the weight of memories, the promise of what could have been, and the undeniable truth that some bonds are simply too strong to be broken.

As I stood there, I knew that no matter where life had taken us, those eyes would forever be imprinted on my heart.

I was still staring, locked into his gaze's embrace when the sound of someone calling my name finally broke me out of trance.

"Uhm... what?"

"It's time to give your speech, Lydie," Tori told me.

"Oh, yeah, right."

"Here," Jack said, plucking the napkins from my hand gently. "I can finish it. You should probably clean your hand, too."

"Yeah, right."

I really was one with words right now.

Quickly, I wiped the cake and frosting off of my hand, grabbed the notecards Tori handed me, and made my way to the front of the bakery to the small podium.

Taking a deep breath, I stepped up to the podium. Earlier, my nerves had threatened to overwhelm me, but now, as I looked out at the sea of friendly faces, a strange calmness settled over me.

As I began to speak, my voice wavered slightly, but the words flowed more easily than I had anticipated. It was a moment of reflection, a celebration of the journey that had led me to this point, a point where my little bakery had become a symbol of love, dedication, and dreams realized.

I cleared my throat, lifted my notecards, and spoke into the microphone before me.

"Ladies and gentlemen, esteemed guests, and dear friends of Beaufort. I stand before you today with a heart filled with gratitude that knows no bounds.

"Twenty years ago, I embarked on a journey that I could never have imagined would lead me to this moment. As I look around at the beauty of this celebration, at the faces that have supported me and cheered me on, I am humbled beyond words."

As I talked, my gaze never left Jack's.

"When I opened *Southern Sweets and Pies*, I was a dreamer with flour on my hands and hope in my heart. Today, to see my bakery on the cover of *Southern Charm and Treats*, to receive countless orders and business, it's a testament not only to my hard work but to the unwavering support of this incredible community.

"I want to express my deepest gratitude to each and every one of you here tonight. From the friends who dropped by for a slice of pie and a chat, to the loyal customers who have stood by me through thick and thin, you have made my dream a reality. Your smiles, your words of encouragement, and your patronage have been the wind beneath my wings.

"I must extend a heartfelt thanks to my family and friends who have stood by me every step of the way.

"Your belief in me, your sacrifices, and your love have given me the strength to push forward even when challenges seemed insurmountable. To Tori and Sam, who put together this incredible celebration, you've orchestrated a masterpiece that has touched my heart deeply.

"But above all, I want to acknowledge the divine presence that has guided me from day one. None of this would have been possible without the grace of God. His hand has been in every recipe, every interaction, and every success that *Southern Sweets and Pies* has enjoyed. With His guidance, I have been able to create not just desserts, but moments of joy and memories that I hope will linger in your hearts.

"As I stand here today, I am reminded of the power of dreams, of hard work, and of the profound impact a community can have on an individual's journey. From the bottom of my heart, thank you.

"Here's to the sweet past, the delicious present, and the delectable future that we will create together."

All around me, the sounds of clapping exploded, but I was distracted by someone specific.

Jack.

I hadn't seen him in so long, hadn't even heard a whisper of his name in years. And yet, here he was, a ghost from the past suddenly made real before my eyes.

How long had he been here? Why hadn't I known he was coming?

A whirlwind of questions spun through my mind, but the answers seemed elusive.

His hair still held some of that sun-kissed glow I remember so well mixing well with the silver, and his smile revealed those charming dimples I had always adored. The years had treated him well, etching a maturity into his features that only made him more handsome. His broad shoulders, the same ones that had once offered me comfort, now seemed to carry a lifetime of experiences.

His gaze was like a warm touch that sent shivers down my spine.

It was surreal, the sensation of time folding in on itself. The memories, the laughter, the dreams we had shared—it was all there, simmering just beneath the surface. I had thought that the love I had once felt for him had faded into a distant memory, a chapter closed long ago.

But now, seeing him again, that love was like an ember reignited, casting a soft glow on the edges of my heart.

As the applause died down, I left the podium and walked through the crowd. Everyone was excited to shake my hand, give me a hug, take a picture with me, but all I could hope for was at the end of the line, Jack would be there waiting for me.

Would I have the chance to talk to him? To catch up on the years that had slipped by? I felt a mixture of excitement and trepidation. The crowd moved, mingling, and I found myself inching closer to where he had stood.

Yet, by the time I got to the end of the crowd, time had passed and Jack was no longer there. I looked around, frantic for one silly moment that maybe I had dreamed him up and he had never actually been there.

If it weren't for the stickiness on my hand from the dessert, I may have just believed it.

Seeing Tori close by, I approached her, asking if she had seen where Jack had gone.

"Oh, that guy from earlier? I don't know. He was here just a moment ago."

Disappointment reigned inside of me.

Why did he leave? Was he embarrassed about the cake incident? Had I ruined our reunion before even getting a chance to enjoy it?

The celebration was in full swing, again, the air humming with laughter, clinking glasses, and the soft strains of music in the background. But amidst the joyful ambiance, my heart couldn't help but feel a strange mixture of confusion and disappointment. Jack's sudden disappearance after my speech had left me bewildered and unprepared for the intensity of emotions that surged within me.

His presence had felt like an anchor, grounding me as I stood before the crowd. But now, as I looked around the bustling bakery, he was nowhere to be found.

Why had he left? What had changed in those few moments?

My mind raced through countless scenarios, each more bewildering than the last.

Perhaps the cake mishap had weighed more heavily on him than I had thought. But that didn't make sense; he had stayed through my entire speech, his gaze never leaving mine. Why would he endure that if he was truly upset?

The more I pondered, the more my heart ached. It was as if a piece of my past had resurfaced only to slip through my fingers once again.

Memories rushed back, flooding my thoughts with fragments of our shared history. We had been high school sweethearts, two young souls entwined in a love that felt like it could conquer any obstacle.

And as I remembered us, I remembered the promise we made to each other.

I couldn't forget the time capsule we had buried in the backyard, our dreams encapsulated in letters, mementos, and promises. It was a ritual, a promise that once our dreams came true, we would find each other again.

Could it be that he was here because of that? Had he achieved his dreams as I had? Was he looking for closure, for answers?

Returning to the throng of guests, I put on a brave face, chatting and mingling as if my heart wasn't aching with unanswered questions. But Jack was always at the back of my mind, his absence like a void I couldn't ignore.

As the night wore on, my thoughts swirled with the memories of our past. The love we had shared, the dreams we had dared to nurture—it all felt like it was alive again, right beneath the surface. The ache I felt in my chest was more than the mere confusion of his departure; it was the resurgence of emotions I thought I had long buried.

The night came to a close, the celebration winding down. I glanced around one last time, hoping against hope to catch a glimpse of him, but he remained elusive. As guests bid their farewells and the bakery quieted, I couldn't escape the weight of what I felt.

As soon as the night was over, I helped the caterers and staff Tori and Sam hired to clean up the store. I knew they were more than capable of doing it themselves, but I liked the monotony of keeping my hands busy as I tried to regulate my emotions.

By the time everything was cleaned, the tables broken down, the podium removed, and the leftover food put away, it was well past midnight, and I was exhausted. After a night like this, I couldn't wait to get home, pour myself a glass of wine, and just relax for a little bit before calling it a night.

Ready to lock up the shop, I gave my thanks to all of the workers as they trickled out. I punched in the digits to the alarm system by the wall and locked the door before I left.

I was just walking along the street to where my car was parked when a figure sitting on a bench stood up and smiled at me.

"Hello, Lydie," he said, smiling.

This time, I couldn't keep the smile from my face as I looked at him.

"Hi, Jack. It's nice to see you again."

Chapter Two

Jack

Moving back to Beaufort felt like a blessing straight from heaven.

Never in my wildest dreams did I think I'd have the chance to call this small, charming South Carolina town home again.

Fate had an uncanny way of playing its hand, as my mother's health took a sharp decline, leaving her unable to live alone. The decision was clear – I needed to be here for her, and so, I found myself back where I once made unforgettable memories.

But amidst the mixed emotions of caregiving, a question haunted my every thought.

Lydie Dawson.

She was still living here, right across from my mother's house – a piece of my past I thought I'd left behind. I hadn't spoken to her since I left for the military years ago.

Would she remember me? Did she even care?

The uncertainty gnawed at me, a constant undercurrent of anxiety that pushed me to seclude myself within my mother's house.

Days turned into weeks, and I found solace in the familiarity of my surroundings while wrestling with the fear of bumping into Lydie.

What if she looked at me with a blank expression, not recognizing the boy who had once given his heart to her? What if our shared memories had faded, lost to the passage of time?

Then, a glimmer of hope appeared in the form of a party invitation – not for me, but for my mother. It was an invitation to a celebration in Lydie's honor, marking the success of her bakery being featured in a popular food magazine.

At that moment, reading the words on the page, it felt like divine intervention.

The article accompanying the invitation held a small interview with Lydie, her words etching themselves into my mind. She spoke about her dreams, her bakery, and how everything she had ever yearned for had come true.

It was in reading her words that I couldn't help but recall the promise we'd made to each other all those years ago.

Once our dreams came true, we would find each other again.

My mother's illness had cast a shadow over our lives, leaving her bedridden and unable to attend the celebration. It was a difficult reality to face, and as I saw her health deteriorate, the weight of responsibility settled heavily on my shoulders. But when the invitation arrived, to attend the celebration in Lydie's honor, a spark of hope ignited within me.

I told myself that I was going for my mother, to convey her congratulations and well wishes to Lydie. It was a noble intention, a way to honor the woman who had raised me with love and sacrifice.

But deep down, I knew there was another reason, a more personal motivation that drove me.

The invitation was like a message from heaven, a sign that fate was offering me a chance I hadn't dared to hope for. It was an opportunity to see Lydie again, to be in her presence once more.

I couldn't ignore the pull I felt, the magnetic force drawing me toward the celebration. It was as if God Himself had orchestrated this moment, a reminder that life was full of twists and turns, second chances, and the rekindling of old flames.

I couldn't let this opportunity slip through my fingers again.

As I walked into the celebration, the atmosphere was charged with excitement. People mingled laughter and conversations filled the air, and in the midst of it all was Lydie, the woman who had ignited a spark in my heart all those years ago. Her presence was a balm for my soul, a reminder of the connection we had shared as children.

The evening arrived, filled with the energy of excited guests and the aroma of delectable pastries. The air hummed with anticipation as I walked through the door, my heart pounding in my chest.

My timing couldn't have been more perfect as Lydie stopped near me to chat with some people.

Her smile, her grace, they held a magnetic power over me. It was as if time had melted away, leaving only the echoes of our shared past and the possibility of a future that was waiting to be explored.

So, I stood there, amidst the crowd, watching her with a mixture of pride, awe, and anticipation. The celebration was a testament to her journey, her dreams realized, and the strength that had carried her through. And as I watched her, I knew that my presence here was not just for my mother, but for myself as well – a chance to rekindle an old flame, to explore a path that God had laid out before us once more.

In watching her, the years melted away, and for a moment, it was as if we were kids again, sharing secrets and dreams beneath the Carolina sun. As I approached her, the concern that she wouldn't remember me faded into insignificance.

Of course, I wasn't expecting to be slapped with cake, but it didn't matter to me, especially not when Lydie's hand grazed my skin.

Because of the nature of my career – Lieutenant Colonel of the 98th Squadron of the U.S. Army – I did not put much priority into being as close with someone as I once was with the woman in front of me.

At first, it took years for me to get over Lydie, to ever think I could love someone else again. Then, when I finally woke up one day and the ache was much smaller, and my days got brighter again, I started throwing myself into work.

I loved my job. I loved the commitment I made to my country.

And for a while, that was enough.

But, like before, I woke up one day and it wasn't. I started to miss what it was like to love someone, and thinking of love, led me to memories of Lydie. I wanted to see her again.

But no memory compared to the feel of her touch, so

when she mopped cake from my face, I felt like I was falling in love all over again.

When she had to break away, my heart ached in my chest.

Watching Lydie climb the podium and stand confidently before the crowd, delivering her speech with grace and passion, was a sight to behold. Her words flowed effortlessly, painting a picture of her journey, her dreams, and the dedication that had led her to this moment.

But what surprised me the most wasn't her words or her achievements – it was the simple act of her touch. It was as if that touch had rekindled dormant sensations, emotions I had long buried beneath the practicalities of life. It was overwhelming, an almost startling reminder of the depth of my feelings for her.

In the last few decades, no one had evoked such a visceral response from me. It was both exhilarating and disconcerting. Love, adoration, and joy surged through me.

As she continued speaking, I found it difficult to tear my gaze away from her.

Our eyes met, and it was as if the rest of the room vanished, leaving just the two of us in a universe of shared memories and unfinished conversations. Her unwavering gaze felt like a lifeline, anchoring me to a time when things were simpler when our connection was unburdened by the complexities of adulthood.

The intensity of the moment amplified as Lydie's speech reached its conclusion.

Applause erupted around us, but I remained locked in that private exchange with her. When she disappeared into the crowd afterward, I realized that the emotional tornado inside me was becoming too much to handle.

I needed air, and space to process the rush of feelings

that had taken me by surprise. So, I stepped outside, the cool night air providing a welcomed contrast to the heated emotions raging within me.

Seated on a bench, I stared into the distance, attempting to gather my thoughts. The mixture of fear and intrigue that Lydie's touch had stirred was both unsettling and thrilling.

It was as if her mere presence had opened a door to a realm of emotions I had long kept locked away.

As I sat there, gazing up at the stars, I couldn't help but wonder if this unexpected reunion was a second chance, an opportunity to explore the unfinished chapters of our story. The emotional turmoil was daunting, but it was also a testament to the depth of what we once shared.

I was locked away in my own mind that I didn't notice Lydie approaching until she was standing right in front of me.

"Hello, Lydie."

After greeting me, she sat on the bench.

The night sky spread out above us like a canvas of twinkling stars, casting a mesmerizing glow over everything. There we sat, side by side, in comfortable silence.

As Lydie's gaze remained fixed on the stars, I couldn't help but steal glances at her.

She was as breathtaking as I remembered – her long, chestnut hair catching the soft light, her eyes a vivid blue that seemed to hold the essence of the ocean.

The soft splatter of freckles across her nose, a detail that had always endeared her to me, was still there. It was a piece of her that time had preserved, a fragment of the girl I had known.

And age, though gentle, had woven its delicate touches across her features, enhancing her beauty in ways I couldn't have foreseen.

The lines around her eyes, etched with laughter and the passage of countless days, told a story of resilience and growth. The gentle crows' feet at the corners of her eyes spoke of years spent cherishing moments, the highs and lows of a life well-lived.

My gaze wandered to the small wrinkle on her forehead, a testament to her determination and the challenges she had faced. It was a feature that hadn't been there when we were kids, but now it was a reminder of the weight of responsibility she had carried in her pursuit of dreams.

Each line on her face was a chapter in her story. It was a reminder of all that she had learned and accomplished, and of the strength and resilience she had shown in the face of adversity. It was also a reminder of her potential and her ability to achieve anything she set her mind to.

Our paths had diverged, leading us down separate roads filled with their own trials and triumphs. Yet, here we were, side by side once more, connected by a shared history.

I cleared my throat, breaking the comfortable silence that had enveloped us. "You know, Lydie, I've always been amazed by your determination," I confessed softly, my voice carrying a weight of sincerity.

Her gaze shifted from the stars to meet mine, her eyes sparkling with a mixture of emotions. "Thank you, Jack. It's been a journey, that's for sure. But I wouldn't trade it for anything."

With a small smile, she turned her attention back to the night sky, and I followed suit. More silence until Lydie looked at me this time.

"Jack?"

"Yeah?"

"When did you come back?"

"About two weeks ago. I'm living with my mom now."

Lydie nodded, sadly. "I heard about her health. I'm very sorry, Jack."

My mother, Vivian, has always been the pillar of my life, the unwavering support that guided me through every twist and turn.

She stood by me when I was just a kid, full of dreams and mischief. Those teenage years were tumultuous, especially after the loss of my father when I was fourteen, but her patience in me never wavered.

As life moved on and my career took me to places far from Beaufort, the distance between us grew. But her presence was always felt, a comforting anchor that reminded me of the values she had instilled in me.

Then, came the news that shattered my heart.

The news that her health was failing, that she needed hospice care for the remaining days of her life. The realization hit me like a tidal wave, and I found myself crumbling beneath its weight, leaving me breathless and lost.

In that moment, all the memories flooded back – the late-night talks, the sacrifices she made to provide for me, the laughter and tears we had shared. And I knew, without a shadow of a doubt, that I had to be there for her, just as she had always been there for me.

Without hesitation, I made the decision to uproot my life. I sold my house in Texas, packed up my belongings, and moved to Beaufort in less than a month. I was coming home, not just to the town that had shaped my childhood, but to be by her side when she needed me the most.

The first time I saw her in that hospital room, a mix of emotions welled up within me – sadness for her declining health, gratitude for her unwavering presence in my life, and a fierce determination to make her remaining days as comfortable as possible.

Chapter Two   19

She was my rock, my guiding light, and now it was my turn to be hers.

"Thank you," I said to Lydie.

"I'm also really sorry about the cake in your face."

I chuckled. "I promise it's fine. It was a very tasty cake."

She laughed, too, and the sound of it was beautiful to my ears.

Too soon, she hooked her purse over her shoulder and stood up. "It's getting late," she said. "I should get home."

I didn't even know how late it was until I looked at my watch and the arrows were pointing closer to the two.

"I'm sorry," I said. "I had no idea how late it was. Would it be okay if I walked you to your car?"

Lydie beamed. "I would like that."

As we rose from the bench, the night around us felt like a tranquil cocoon. The air was crisp, the sky a dark canvas sprinkled with stars, and as we walked side by side, it was as though time itself had slowed down just for us. I couldn't help but be captivated by the ease with which we fell into step together.

Though the hour was late and both of us were tired from the festivities, we didn't quicken our pace. Instead, we sauntered forward, our steps unhurried as if we were savoring the minutes slipping through our fingers.

Shoulder to shoulder, our arms hung at our sides. My mind wandered in those quiet moments, thoughts swirling like leaves caught in a gentle breeze. A burning curiosity tugged at me: *how simple it would be to move my hand a fraction closer, to let our fingers touch.*

I yearned to feel the warmth of her skin against mine.

But fear, and a gnawing doubt, held me back. We had drifted apart for so many years, and in that chasm of separation, I questioned whether I still had the right to touch her, to reach out and grasp the intangible threads of our shared history.

Would she welcome the contact, or would my touch be an intrusion, a reminder of the past that had been left behind?

With hesitant resolve, I decided to test the waters, to gauge her response. I let my index finger break away from the rest, its tip grazing the back of her hand in a feather-light caress. The gasp that escaped her lips was like music to my ears, a joyful melody that echoed the sentiment in my heart.

Encouraged by her reaction, I found the courage to take a bolder step.

My fingers reached out, inching toward hers, longing to make that connection. And then, as my fingertips were on the verge of brushing hers, we arrived at her car. The abrupt halt felt like a suspended moment in time, life conspiring to keep us in this liminal space.

Standing by her car, the weight of the moment pressed upon me. The night had been magical, a reconnection I had never imagined possible. But now, faced with the reality of parting ways once more, I felt a knot of unease twist in my stomach. I couldn't let this be the end, not after feeling the rush of emotions and shared history that had flowed between us.

As Lydie turned to face me, her eyes searching mine, I sensed that she was grappling with similar thoughts. We stood in silence, an unspoken understanding hanging in the air like a delicate thread. I wanted to ask her if we could see each other again if we could pick up the fragments of our relationship and weave them back into something beautiful. But the words eluded me, caught in the tangle of my emotions.

In that moment, a thought – a lifeline – flickered in my mind, as if placed there by God Himself.

I remembered the time capsule we had buried in her backyard all those years ago. The memory surged within me, bittersweet and laden with nostalgia. We had promised to open it thirty years from the last day we saw each other. I had forgotten about it, time slipping through my fingers in the rush of life.

But did she remember? Had she kept that promise?

My heart raced at the prospect, the idea that something from our past could be a bridge to our future. It was as if fate had orchestrated this moment, nudging me toward a way to continue our connection.

Taking a deep breath, I met her gaze with a mixture of hope and uncertainty. "Lydie, do you remember the time capsule we buried in your backyard?" The words tumbled out, laced with the weight of years gone by.

Recognition flickered in her eyes, followed by a thoughtful smile. "Of course I remember, Jack."

Elated surprise washed over me. "Did... did you dig it up?"

"No, I thought about it, but it felt wrong not to do it with you beside me."

Warmth at her words spread through me. She didn't want to open it without me. She wanted me to be there with her.

"Lydie, would you consider opening the time capsule with me?" I asked, my voice steady despite all of the emotions swirling in my stomach.

A spark of excitement lit up in her eyes, her smile mirroring my own. "I would love that, Jack. It's a beautiful idea."

As we parted ways for the night, we exchanged our

numbers and promised to see each other in the next couple of days. I couldn't help but feel a renewed sense of hope.

The time capsule wasn't just a buried container – it was a symbol of our enduring bond, a declaration of love, friendship, and memories that had held us together all these years.

Chapter Three

Lydie

I can't believe he remembers the time capsule.

Driving home, I had no idea that tonight would even remotely turn out the way it did. The night had been filled with surprises, from his presence at the celebration to the ease with which we had reconnected after so many years apart. But nothing had caught me off guard quite like his mention of the time capsule we had buried so long ago.

As the engine hummed softly, my thoughts drifted to that small container hidden beneath the earth. It felt like a relic from a different lifetime, a testament to the dreams and promises we had made as two lovestruck kids.

Yet, as I tried to recall what I had placed inside the time capsule, I found myself struggling. The memories were hazy, like fragments of a dream slipping through my fingers.

At the time, those items had been the most important things I owned, a snapshot of my hopes and dreams.

A vague memory of me folding a letter with my clumsy, teenage handwriting, a letter to my future self, surfaced in my thoughts. Whatever words the letter contained, I had poured my heart into them, expressing my dreams and aspirations with an innocence that only a young heart could possess.

As I navigated the streets, I couldn't shake the feelings that had settled over me – the time capsule represented a link to my past, a portal to the dreams and aspirations that had driven me forward. It was a reminder of the innocence I had once carried.

But now, as an adult facing the challenges of reality, those dreams had evolved, transformed by the experiences that had shaped me. I wondered if the contents of the time capsule would still resonate with who I had become, or if they would feel like old antiques from a different lifetime.

As I pulled into my driveway, the weight of the time capsule lingered in my thoughts. I knew that opening it again with Jack would be a journey into the past, a chance to reflect on the dreams that had led us to this point.

Back in the quiet cocoon of my house, the energy of the night's festivities still thrummed through me.

I poured myself a glass of wine, letting the rich, velvety liquid cascade into the glass. With my glass in hand, I kicked off my heels, peeled off the blouse over my tank top, and finally sighed, letting the chaos of today peel away like a second skin.

I knew it was late, that sleep should be beckoning me to bed, but my mind was a tangled knot and there was no way I would be able to find peace enough to close my eyes and slumber.

Instead, I decided to take a walk down memory lane. I ventured into the heart of my home, in search of my high school yearbook from '72. The book had collected a thin layer of dust, a nod to the decades that had passed since I last opened its pages.

With gentle fingers, I pulled it down from the shelf as if it were a treasure that needed to be handled gently.

Seated on the floor, cross-legged and bathed in the soft glow of a lamp, I gingerly opened the yearbook. Each turn of the page felt like a journey back in time. Laughter, dreams, and a sense of boundless possibilities leapt off the pages, transporting me to a time when life was simpler.

And then, there it was – an image that made my heart skip a beat. A photograph of Jack and me, captured on a night that had etched itself into my soul.

In the Prom photograph, we stood side by side, beaming with a radiance that only young love could bestow. I wore a gown that felt like a dream come true, and Jack, well, he looked every bit the dashing man that he was. We were crowned King and Queen, a moment that had felt like magic unfolding before our eyes.

Staring at that image, I was transported back to that night, to the sensation of his hand in mine as we danced, the whispers of dreams shared beneath the stars, the feeling that anything was possible. We were young, naive, and hopeful that life would not be strong enough to separate us.

As I sat there, the weight of the yearbook in my hands, memories unfurled like a fragile tapestry before my mind's eye. And yet, beneath the surface of nostalgia, there was a pang in my heart, a dull ache that I couldn't ignore.

. . .

My gaze shifted from the smiling faces in the photo to their hands, each of their ring fingers adorned with a simple, unassuming band.

A promise ring – a symbol of a commitment made in the innocence of youth, a vow to love and cherish each other always. I couldn't help but trace the contours of the ring in the image with my fingertip, each movement sending a tremor of emotion through me.

The memory of that moment was etched into my heart, as vivid and poignant as the day it had happened.

It was a sun-drenched afternoon, the world painted in hues of gold and possibility. Jack and I had been sitting by the edge of the lake, the water reflecting the sky like a mirror. With laughter dancing on our lips, we had slipped matching rings onto each other's fingers, sealing a promise that had felt like the most natural thing in the world.

But now, as I sat here alone, the echo of that promise reverberated within me. It was a whisper from the past, a reminder of a love that had been pure and true. And yet, our paths had diverged, life had thrown its twists and turns, and that promise had vanished into the mists of time.

The ache in my heart wasn't just from the memory of the breakup, but from the realization that even after all these years, my feelings for Jack hadn't truly subsided.

I had thrown myself into my dreams, my goals, my career, always believing that putting myself first was the right path. And yet, I couldn't deny that no one else had ever compared to Jack.

I had tried to move on, convinced that the choices I had made were the right ones. I hadn't dated, hadn't allowed myself to get close to anyone in a way that could jeopardize the walls I had built. And while I had succeeded in achieving many of my dreams, that ache remained – a reminder that deep down, I had always known that Jack was the one God had chosen for me.

As I stared at the promise ring, I couldn't escape the shadows of doubt that crept in.

Had I made the right choices? Had I chosen the path of self-preservation over the path of love?

The ache in my heart was both bittersweet and cathartic.

The heartbreak was a reminder of the pain and sorrow that had once consumed me, the tears I had shed in the dark of night as I struggled with the uncertainty of our future, a reminder of the time when I thought I would never be happy again, when I thought that the pain would never go away.

It was also a reminder of my strength and resilience, of how I had overcome the torment and come out stronger on the other side.

With a heavy heart, I set the yearbook aside, its pages filled with memories that held both joy and sorrow.

All of the sudden, I felt overwhelmingly exhausted, so I drank the last of my wine from the glass and headed to my bedroom.

As I lay down on my bed, the moon casting a soft glow through the window, I knew that tomorrow was a new day, a chance to face the echoes of the past and the possibilities of the future.

And as I drifted into sleep, my thoughts lingered on the promises we had made and the choices we had taken – a tapestry of emotions that painted the canvas of my heart.

A couple of days later, the morning sun filtered through the curtains, casting a warm glow across my room. After the whirlwind of emotions that had consumed me the previous day, I had spent most of Sunday sleeping and recharging.

But as Monday arrived, duty called, and I knew it was time to dive back into the rhythm of life.

The bakery had never been busier.

The news of being featured on the cover of a renowned food magazine had ignited a frenzy of interest. People from near and far were flocking to the store, eager to taste the creations that had captured the magazine's attention. Some came for the delectable desserts, while others simply wanted a glimpse of the woman behind the bakery's success – me.

The appreciation was overwhelming, a symphony of compliments and applause that echoed in the air. I couldn't help but be delighted by the attention, the realization that my hard work was paying off in ways I had never imagined. The bakery, once a cozy haven of my culinary dreams, had transformed into a bustling hub of activity.

But with the surge in popularity came the challenges.

The demands had grown exponentially, and I found myself stretched thin between the front of the bakery and the kitchen where my heart truly belonged. Before, the small team I had – one cashier and one delivery person – had been sufficient. We had managed to run the bakery together, handling orders and interactions with customers. But now, as orders flooded in and lines formed, I had to expand my team.

Hiring additional staff was both a necessity and a challenge. It meant relinquishing some control over the day-to-day operations, trusting others to uphold the standards I had set. The dynamics of the bakery were shifting, transforming from a closely-knit trio to a larger, bustling ensemble. It was an adjustment, a dance of balance between delegation and preserving the essence of what had made *Southern Treats and Pies*.

And yet, amidst the hustle and bustle, I couldn't deny the respite that the bakery provided.

It was my sanctuary, a place where I could lose myself in the alchemy of creating sugary delights. It was a refuge from the echoing thoughts of Jack that had haunted me since our reunion.

While frosting cupcakes and kneading dough, I could focus on the task at hand, letting the motions of baking serve as a balm for my racing thoughts. The rhythm of the kitchen, the scent of vanilla and butter, they became my safe space from the emotional maelstrom that had gripped me.

The bakery was my cocoon, a place where I could lose myself in the intricacies of my craft.

As I glanced at the clock, I realized it was mid-afternoon. The bakery was still abuzz with activity, customers coming and going, savoring the fruits of my labor, but most of the early morning craziness was gone. I wiped my hands on my apron and took a deep breath, letting the scent of freshly baked goods fill my senses. It was moments like these that reminded me why I had poured my heart and soul into this endeavor.

Folding my apron in my hand as I walked, I approached the young girl I had hired as one of my cashiers.

"Hey, Sarah, do you mind holding down the fort for a couple of hours?" I asked her. "I promised my niece I'd get lunch with her today."

Sarah smiled, brightly. "No problem! Thankfully, most of the rush is gone for the day. Woo!"

I chuckled at her enthusiasm. "Well, now, don't jinx us. Oh, I have some more lemon squares that could be put in the display. Would you mind setting those up? Feel free to have one while you work."

"Oh, yes! I love your lemon squares."

I winked at her. "I know, that's why I offered."

"Have a good lunch!" she called out, right before the door of the bakery closed behind me.

The brisk walk to the restaurant was a welcome change of pace from the bustling bakery. Just a short distance away, I reached the cozy French bistro where I had arranged to meet Tori.

As I stepped inside the bistro, the ambiance enveloped me – soft lighting, the soothing murmur of conversation, and the faint aroma of freshly baked bread. I scanned the room and soon spotted Tori, a vision of contentment. She sat there, a radiant smile on her face, with Adam on her lap, bouncing him up and down. The sound of his giggles, like tinkling bells, filled the air even before I reached their table.

Tori looked up, her eyes alight with joy as they met mine. "Lydie, you made it!" she exclaimed.

"Of course, I wouldn't miss it," I replied, the corners of my mouth lifting as I approached the table. The sight of Adam's cherubic face, his infectious laughter, brought an immediate surge of happiness to my heart.

As I took a seat across from Tori, Adam's giggles continued to weave their magic. I marveled at the scene before me – a miracle in the journey Tori had embarked upon since that fateful summer she came to Beaufort. It had been a time of healing, of finding solace and guidance when she needed it most.

Looking at Tori now, I saw a woman who had blossomed in the embrace of love and faith. Her eyes sparkled with a genuine happiness, a light that had once been dimmed by life's challenges. She had not only found love –

a man who cherished her for who she was – but had also become a mother to precious little Adam.

I leaned forward, my voice tender as I spoke to Adam, who regarded me with curious, wide eyes. "Well, hello there, little man," I cooed.

Adam's giggles escalated, his tiny hands reaching out to wrap around my fingers.

Tori's gaze held a mixture of pride and gratitude as she watched her son. "He's quite the bundle of energy," she said, her voice infused with a mother's fondness. "Being a mom has been the most incredible journey. I never imagined my life would turn out like this."

I nodded, my heart swelling with happiness for Tori. Her journey had been one of growth, of embracing the unexpected twists and turns that life had presented. She had faced challenges with unwavering strength and had emerged stronger, her heart open to the blessings that came her way.

"It's truly amazing to see how far you've come," I said, my voice sincere. "You've built a beautiful family, Tori. Adam is lucky to have you as his mom."

Tori's smile deepened, her gaze filled with a sense of fulfillment. "And I owe so much of it to you, Lydie," she said, her voice carrying a touch of emotion. "You took me in, you guided me, and you showed me that even in the midst of life's storms, there's always a ray of hope."

As I gazed at Tori, the bond we had formed over the years felt as strong as ever. She had grown into a woman who embraced life with undeterred courage, and her journey had brought a renewed sense of purpose to my own life. In her and Adam, I saw the beauty of unexpected blessings and the enduring willpower of the human spirit.

Once the server arrived at our table, I held the energetic

toddler in my own lap so that Tori could rummage through her diaper bag for wet wipes.

"I'd like a cup of French onion soup with a slice of baguette bread. A garden salad with French dressing would also be lovely," I told the server. "A glass of sweet sun tea, too, please."

"I'll have the salmon with the seasonal vegetables, and this little guy here will probably just take a chocolate croissant," Tori informed, looking quickly over the menu. "He ate once he got up from his nap a little over an hour ago, so he shouldn't be too hungry. I'll also have the sun tea, please."

As soon as the teas were placed in front of us, I thanked the server graciously. I didn't know how thirsty I was until the straw was between my lips and I was drinking in the sugary deliciousness. It was like my exhausted brain mentally sighed, enjoying the energy only artificial sugars could provide, and I sighed aloud. By the time I was done sipping from the straw, I had drunk most of it already.

"Wow, hard day at work?" Tori teased.

"More like a hard last couple of days," I confessed.

Tori raised an eyebrow. "Oh, how so?"

For a moment, I hesitated. A part of me – the part that always chose perseverance over everything else – didn't want to voice my strenuous thoughts. However, the other part of me felt like I was drowning in my own emotional turmoil, and I needed someone to listen to me.

So there, as I sat across from Tori, the cozy ambiance of the restaurant enveloping us, I found myself opening up about Jack.

I recounted the time we had spent together as children, the promises we had made to always love each other, and the years that had passed since we had last seen each other.

She listened attentively as I spoke about the time capsule, a symbol of our shared past, and how Jack mentioned we should open it together. I confessed the uncertainty that had taken root in my heart – the fear that perhaps he didn't feel the same way, that the years apart might have dulled the connection between us.

When I was finished, Tori's eyes were wide, and her mouth slightly agape. "Wow," she breathed out, "this is like the best romance book ever written. I'm officially jealous. No one ever shared a time capsule with me."

I couldn't help but laugh. "Don't get too excited, I don't even remember what's inside of it."

"That's even better!" Tori exclaimed, happily. "All the more reason to dig it up with him. You guys can relive the memories of everything inside together, and fall in love all over again. Oh, it's so romantic. I have chills. *Literal* chills."

"Okay, before you call the Hallmark channel, I should at least invite him over first, don't you think?"

"Yes, do it now. Use my phone."

Laughing, I shook my head, pushing the phone she had extended out to me back to her. "I think I should do it later when I have more privacy."

Tori pouted. "Okay, I guess you're right, but if everything turns out perfect – which I think it will – you best believe I'm calling Hallmark right away."

Chapter Four

Jack

In the days that followed our reunion, my thoughts were consumed by Lydie. The memory of her smile, the sound of her laughter, and the warmth of her presence lingered in my mind like an irresistible melody. But despite our exchange of contact information and the promise to open the time capsule together, Lydie has not reached out.

In the midst of this emotional tug-of-war, the responsibilities of caring for my mother provided a grounding force.

Viv's health had taken a sharp decline, and I was now her primary caregiver. The roles had reversed – the man who once relied on his mother for guidance and support was now the one ensuring her well-being. I attended to her needs, cooking, cleaning, and making sure she took her medication on time. It was a labor of love, a way to repay her for the years of selfless devotion she had given me.

The days were long, filled with tasks and routines, and yet, amid the busyness, my thoughts would inevitably drift back to Lydie. The anticipation of her call or message became a constant presence. I found myself checking my phone more often than I'd like to admit, my heart skipping a beat each time a notification lit up the screen

As I sat by my mother's side, reading to her or simply holding her hand, my mind would wander to Lydie. I wondered what she was doing, whether she was thinking of me as much as I was thinking of her.

But as the days passed, doubt began to creep in.

Had I misread her signals? Was I just a passing figure in her life, a reminder of a distant past? The uncertainty gnawed at me, a persistent ache that no amount of busyness could soothe. I wanted to reach out, to hear her voice, to see if the spark we had ignited at the party could grow into something more.

Alas, the fear of rejection paralyzed me. What if I reached out and she didn't feel the same way? What if our connection had been a fleeting moment, destined to fade into the background of our lives once more? It was a vulnerability I hadn't felt in years, a reminder of the raw emotions that come with opening your heart to another.

Tuesday evening, as I sat by the window, watching the sun dip below the horizon, a message notification finally broke the silence. My heart raced as I unlocked my phone, the screen illuminating with her name.

Lydie.

I answered the phone on the second ring. "Hello?"

"Hi, Jack. I was wondering if you wanted to come over tomorrow morning. I'm free, and we can finally dig up that time capsule."

There were not enough words in the English dictionary that could express how I was feeling.

"Yes! Uhm... I mean, yes, I would love that."

Through the receiver of my phone, I heard her chuckle. "Great. I'll make us some breakfast."

"Great," I said, then we hung up.

After hanging up with Lydie, I felt a rush of excitement that carried me through the rest of the day. It was as if a new energy had awakened within me, a sense of purpose and anticipation for what lay ahead.

My mother noticed the change in my demeanor, and her laughter filled the room as she playfully questioned the source of my newfound giddiness.

"Jack, what's got you walking on air?" she asked, a twinkle in her eyes as she looked at me.

I couldn't help but grin like a fool. "Mom, I have some exciting news. I connected with Lydie, and we're actually going to meet tomorrow morning."

Her eyebrows shot up in pleasant surprise. "Is that so? Aren't you full of surprises?"

I chuckled, my heart dancing with excitement. "I know, it's kind of unexpected, but I'm really looking forward to it."

As we sat in the cozy living room, I explained to her the details of our plan. A meeting, a chance to catch up, to open the time capsule that had held so many memories of our past. My mother's warmth and understanding were a comforting presence, and I felt grateful to have her by my side.

She smiled knowingly. "I think it's wonderful, Jack. And don't worry about me, I'll be perfectly fine. Marcel, my nurse, is stopping by in the morning."

Her reassurance was a balm to my heart. Taking care of her had become second nature, a role that I embraced with love and dedication. I had worried about leaving her, even for a short while, so it was comforting to know Marcel would be here before I left.

"I'm glad to hear that, Mom," I replied, a mixture of relief and excitement in my voice. "And you know, meeting with Lydie is not just about catching up. It's, well, it's a bit more than that."

My mother's smile was gentle and knowing. "I'm happy for you, Jack. You deserve happiness, and if Lydie can bring that into your life, then I'm all for it."

Her support meant the world to me. But what she said next caught me off guard, reminding me of the kind of person Lydie was.

"I've always liked Lydie," my mother continued, her voice soft with fondness. "She's such a good woman. She'd always come over during the summer and offer to mow my lawn, and she always stops by at least once a week to bring me one of her delicious pecan pies. I know she hasn't in the last couple of weeks because of how busy she is, but I do love those pies."

A warmth filled my chest as I thought about Lydie's kindness and generosity.

"She hasn't changed a bit." I confirmed with myself. "She's still that same caring and selfless person."

My mother nodded, her expression thoughtful. "It sounds like you two have a lot to catch up on tomorrow. Maybe this meeting will be the start of something beautiful."

As I retired to bed that night, the excitement and anticipation in my heart were matched only by the gratitude I felt for the support of the woman who had always been there for me – my mother.

. . .

The next morning, I tried to prepare for the day ahead, and as I stood in front of my closet, I couldn't help but feel a wave of annoyance wash over me. Flannel shirts dominated the space, evidence of my lack of variety in the wardrobe department. I only ever bought clothes for comfort and practicality – not for dates and good impressions.

With a sigh, I sifted through the hangers, seeking something that would exude a more put-together vibe.

"Ugh! Why is this so hard?" I groaned into my clothes.

After what felt like an eternity, I settled on a classic button-down shirt and a pair of dark jeans. It was a simple choice, but at least it showed a hint of the muscles I had developed over the years. I laid them out on my bed and grabbed a towel for the bathroom.

After my shower, I carefully shaved my facial hair, wanting to look polished and well-groomed. I applied my best cologne, the one I usually saved for special occasions.

As I stood before the mirror, I couldn't help but hope that I was presentable enough. Not knowing was really making me more nervous than I ought to be.

Downstairs, the hospice nurse, Marcel, arrived. I greeted him with a nod, appreciating his presence and the care he provided for my mother. I quickly briefed him on her status – meds taken, breakfast eaten, and now in the sunroom enjoying some television.

"You're looking quite nice today," Marcel remarked, his tone casual but sincere.

His compliment caught me off guard, and a hint of insecurity crept in. "Really? You think so?"

Marcel chuckled, shaking his head. "You seem a bit nervous. Big date?"

He had no idea. "Uhm. I don't think we really discussed whether it was a date or not."

"Well, date or not, you look good. Just remember to be yourself. After all, she agreed to meet you because she already likes you."

"That's exactly what I told him!" my mother called out, her words laced with a touch of playful teasing.

I rolled my eyes. "I didn't disagree with you!" I called back to her.

I couldn't help but laugh, feeling a bit ganged up on by the two of them.

With a final nod of thanks to Marcel and a wave toward my mother, I headed for the door.

As I stepped outside, the sun warmed my skin. The nerves were still there, but they were accompanied by a deep sense of gratitude for the support of those around me.

Walking across the street to Lydie's house, I was overpowered with a strong sense of familiarity. The house she lived in was the same one she had grown up in – a beautiful home that held a lifetime of memories. It was a place that had witnessed our shared moments, a backdrop to the stolen kisses and secret glances we had exchanged as teens.

I couldn't help but smile as I remembered the times we had shared in that backyard. Hidden from the watchful eyes of her parents, we had cherished our moments of closeness, feeling the thrill of young love.

The house itself seemed to hold the echoes of our past, a reminder of the connection we had forged in our youth.

Taking a deep breath, I raised my hand to knock on the door, my heart beating so loudly in the cavity of my chest that the moment Lydie opened the door, I was so sure she could hear it.

"Hi, Jack! Come on in!" she greeted me, smiling brightly.

As I stepped through the threshold of Lydie's home, a sense of newness mingled with a profound comfort.

Over the years, she had transformed the space into something that felt uniquely her own. The decor was different from what I remembered, but it was easy to see the love and thought she had poured into every corner.

Plants were on almost every surface, lending a touch of greenery and life to the rooms. Cushions were scattered strategically, inviting guests to sink into their embrace. The walls were adorned with picture frames, each containing snapshots of moments that had shaped her life. The memorabilia told a story of her journey – achievements, travels, and cherished memories.

As I made my way further into the house, I was greeted by the presence of an old, black, fluffy cat.

"You have a cat?" I asked, excited. I always had a soft spot for those furry creatures.

Lydie introduced him as Gus, explaining that she was babysitting him for the week. Apparently, his owner's other sitter had backed out last minute, leaving Gus in need of care.

Lydie's affection for animals was evident as she talked about him, mentioning that he was diabetic and required a strict feeding schedule. She had a way with him, scratching his chin and making him purr contentedly.

"He's sweet, isn't he?" Lydie smiled, looking down at the puffball. "I've always loved cats. Maybe having Gus around will inspire me to adopt one for myself."

After giving Gus a round of well-deserved pets and love, the inviting aroma of breakfast wafted through the air, drawing my attention to the spread she had prepared – a platter of Eggs Benedict, my favorite, accompanied by bacon, ham, waffles, toast, and a pot of rich coffee that smelled heavenly.

"I didn't know how hungry you'd be," she admitted with a sheepish grin. "I might have cooked more than I meant to. Nervous energy, I guess."

The confession made her even more endearing in my eyes.

"I can relate." I chuckled, my heart warmed by her vulnerability. "I spent way too much time in front of my closet this morning, trying to pick out an outfit."

Her laughter was like music, a melody that resonated in the room. It was comforting to know that we both shared a touch of nervousness, a reminder that this meeting held significance for both of us. As she reassured me that I looked nice, I couldn't help but smile in return.

"You also look very beautiful," I told her.

And, she did. She was wearing a white peplum blouse with blue daisies printed on the bottom and a pair of dark jeans that flared at her ankles. Her hair was pulled back into a ponytail, and she wore a simple gold cross around her neck.

Sitting across from Lydie, the scent of a delicious breakfast filling the air, I couldn't help but feel a sense of contentment come over me. The morning sunlight filtered through the windows, casting a warm glow over the room.

As we dug into the spread she had prepared, our conversation flowed naturally.

I shared about my role as a Lieutenant in the army, the bonds I had formed with my platoon that felt more like family than colleagues. I spoke about the sense of duty that had driven me to serve, the conviction that I was following a path God had intended for me. I told her about the challenges and triumphs, the weight of responsibility, and the camaraderie that had sustained me.

"Those soldiers, they mean everything to me," I said, my voice tinged with emotion. "I'd do anything for them."

Lydie listened attentively, her gaze reflecting understanding and respect.

"After culinary school in New York, I worked as a sous chef in the city for five years," Lydie began. "But I realized that wasn't where my heart belonged. I had a dream to open my own bakery, so I went back to my parents and talked to them about it. They loaned me the money I needed, and I moved back to Beaufort to pursue my dream."

Her story resonated with me, her courage to chase her dream despite challenges mirroring my own journey. She described the early days of her bakery, the struggles and doubts that clouded her path. But perseverance prevailed, and slowly, she found her footing. Her eyes lit up as she mentioned the moment she made enough money to repay her parents, a milestone that marked the turning point in her journey.

"It's surreal, really. I believe Jesus shaped my future, but I couldn't have done it without the support of my parents and the people who believed in me."

Her gratitude was palpable, and I couldn't help but be awed by the way she acknowledged the importance of the people who had stood by her side. Her connection to her faith was evident, a guiding force that had shaped her path and her outlook on life.

"It's amazing to see how much you appreciate the people who've been there for you," I said, a sense of admiration in my tone. "And your faith is something truly inspiring."

Lydie's eyes met mine, a gentle smile curving her lips.

"Thank you, Jack. My faith is everything to me. It's what keeps me grounded and gives me strength."

Once our breakfast was finished, Lydie and I stepped out into the backyard. Two shovels leaned against her patio furniture, and she held out a tube of sunscreen with a smile. I thanked her and applied the sunscreen, soaking in the warmth of the day.

As we looked out at her picturesque lawn, I couldn't help but feel a pang of concern. "Are you sure you're okay with digging holes?" I asked.

Lydie chuckled, her eyes sparkling. "Grass grows back, Jack. Besides, this is a mission to uncover our past. It's worth a little disruption."

With a determined nod, we each grabbed a shovel, ready to embark on our quest to find the buried time capsule.

The only problem was, neither of us could remember the exact spot where we had buried it all those years ago. We dug holes side by side, exchanging teasing banter about the irony of forgetting the location of something so significant.

"I could have sworn it was over here," Lydie said after what felt like our tenth hole, her hands on her hips and a smudge of dirt on her nose.

I reached over and swiped the dirt from her nose with my fingertip. "That's what you said about the last ten holes we dug."

Hours seemed to slip by as we worked, and eventually, we took a break. Lydie whipped up a quick lunch of sandwiches, and she offered me a beer, which I gladly accepted. We sat on her patio, gazing out at the lake in companionable silence.

Amid the comfortable stillness, Lydie's voice broke the

quiet. "You know, I have a vivid memory of us from back when my parents owned this house."

I turned to her, curious. "What memory is that?"

She smiled, her eyes distant as she recalled. "They used to have a hammock strung up between those two trees near the water's edge." She pointed to two large trees growing near the dock. "After the stress of school, you and I would crawl into it and take naps."

My heart skipped a beat as her words unlocked a flood of memories. An image of us lazing in that hammock came to me suddenly. She would usually bring a book out with her: Wuthering Heights, Jane Eyre, The Awakening, anything really, and she would lay at the other end of the hammock while I rubbed her feet. She was a cheerleader and her practices were usually grueling on her, so I always offered her massages back then.

We would stay in that hammock for hours until her parents came outside and called us inside for dinner or to tell me to go home.

I loved that hammock.

I gasped, realization dawning on me. "Lydie, I remember where the capsule is buried."

Her eyes widened in surprise. "You do?"

I nodded, excitement bubbling within me. "Yes, we buried it under the hammock."

A mixture of astonishment and delight painted her features, and I couldn't help but feel a surge of triumph. The memory had resurfaced, leading us to the very spot where we had hidden our promises to each other.

Lydie's smile was infectious. "I can't believe I forgot that! What are we waiting for? Let's go uncover our little time capsule."

We got back to work with renewed energy, our shovels

hitting the ground with purpose. As the sun dipped lower in the sky, our efforts were rewarded. The sound of metal meeting metal echoed in the air as the blade of the shovel struck something solid.

With eager anticipation, we carefully unearthed the time capsule. It was weathered by time, but as we opened it, the contents held a treasure trove of memories – faded photographs, trinkets, and a note that held the essence of our promises to each other.

Our journey had come full circle, from childhood friends to this moment of rediscovery.

And as Lydie and I looked at each other, a shared understanding passed between us – that sometimes, life gives us the chance to reclaim what was lost, to rekindle a connection that had always been waiting for us to find.

Chapter Five

Lydie

Standing there with Jack, the old tin lunch box in his hands, my heart beat heavily in my chest.

We were about to open the time capsule we had buried so many years ago, a relic from our youth that held the memories of our dreams, our love, and our promises.

As Jack popped the lid open, a rush of exhilaration surged through me. Inside were faded polaroids, capturing moments frozen in time—us and our friends during our senior year, smiles and laughter frozen in those fleeting instants.

"Oh, look!" Jack beamed, looking down at a photo of him with the football team. "This was right after they named me captain that year. George" his old best friend "and I got so dru... I mean, we went for milkshakes and then went straight home."

I raised an eyebrow at him and pursed my lips in a way that told him I didn't believe him for one second.

"Oh, really, milkshakes, 'Jack Daniels' Weston?" I questioned, using his old nickname from our school days just to tease him.

It made me laugh to see the embarrassment on his face.

"I was young and stupid. I don't drink like that anymore," he admitted, shame crossing his face. "I definitely made my parents worry."

The way his face saddened as he said that made me wonder if he was thinking of his mother's current health.

I reached across the space and laid my hand gently on his knee. When his gaze met mine, I said, "Hey, your mom knows you love her. And kids, they always cause their parents' grief here and there. Remember when I was sixteen and I dyed my hair that awful red color?" Oh, it was truly terrible. The color didn't fit my complexion at all, and my hair was short so it looked like I was constantly wearing a red helmet. "My mom almost fainted when she saw me for the first time."

"I do remember. I kinda liked it. You looked like MJ from the *Spiderman* comics."

I couldn't help it, I smiled at the compliment because I knew how much those comics were a big part of Jack's life when we were younger.

We continued to peruse the contents of the capsule. My fingers brushed over a handful of dried flower petals — remnants of the bouquet I had carried at prom. I could almost smell the fragrant memories they held.

But it was the sight of our promise rings that tugged at the strings of my heart the most. Delicate silver bands, a gift Jack had given me after Homecoming of '72.

We had just been escorted on the field as the King

and Queen. I remembered that day mostly because of how he had looked at me with those steely gray eyes, full of determination, and asked if I would marry him one day. I had said yes, without hesitation, believing in the depths of my heart that our future was unshakeable.

And now, holding that ring in my hand, it felt like a lifetime ago that I had made that vow. We were just kids then, innocent and full of dreams, with the world stretched out before us.

Back then, I had been so ready to marry Jack, to build a life together that was overflowing with love and nurture. I couldn't have imagined it any other way.

But Jesus has a way of steering us down unexpected paths, teaching us lessons we hadn't anticipated. The separation that had come between us — thirty-four years to be exact — was a hard lesson, one that I had eventually come to accept.

I had come to believe that Jesus, in His wisdom, knew that we weren't ready for that future. Our paths had diverged, and it wasn't an easy road, but it had shaped me into the person I was today.

The person who stood here with Jack, years later, as we revisited the relics of our past.

As I glanced at Jack, I saw a man who had also been shaped by his own journey, his experiences etched into the lines on his face and the wisdom in his eyes. Old feelings were resurfacing, but I knew that just because those feelings existed didn't necessarily mean we were right for each other anymore.

We had grown up, evolved, and perhaps become different people. Our lives had been colored by experiences and lessons that were unique to each of us. While it was tempting to let the past sweep me away, I couldn't ignore the reality of the present.

Jack continued to explore, his eyes lighting up when he came across two small envelopes held together by a baby blue satin ribbon.

"Our love letters!" I exclaimed, happily, remembering them immediately.

At the time we were preparing to bury this capsule, we had agreed to write each other a love letter to open on our future wedding day. On the ribbon, there was a tag with my handwriting. Jack read it aloud. "If we are meant to be together, we vow to open these letters and read them to each other on our very special day."

We both chuckled at the innocence of it.

"Should we read them?" I asked.

Jack was shaking his head. "No, I think maybe we should wait? I don't know, it just doesn't feel right to open them right now."

"I agree." So, instead of opening them, we tucked them carefully back into the box.

"We'll open them," Jack said, looking at me, full of meaning, "one day."

My heart felt like it was swelling inside of my chest. "Yes, one day."

As we closed the time capsule once again, I met Jack's gaze, and a silent understanding passed between us. The promise ring may have represented a vow made by two young hearts, but life had taught us that vows could change, transform, and even be replaced by new promises that were truer to who we had become.

When I looked at Jack, I couldn't help but smile, grateful for the chance to reconnect. Our paths had taken us far from where we had once been, but as we moved forward, I knew that our past, though cherished, would not determine our future.

"Lydie?"

"Yes, Jack?"

"Would you like to go on a date with me?"

"Yes." I couldn't keep the blush from my cheeks. "I would love that."

I was on Cloud Nine.

* * *

The next day, the morning sun streamed through my window, painting the room in a soft glow that forced me to reluctantly emerge from under my cozy sheets.

Panic surged through me as I glanced at the clock and realized I had overslept.

"Oh, crapsickles!"

I rushed to the kitchen, but my sense of urgency shifted when I spotted Gus, blinking up at me from his food bowl. I had almost forgotten that he was staying with me. I checked to make sure he had enough food and prepared his insulin, taking a moment to give him a reassuring pat.

With Gus taken care of, I turned my attention back to the whirlwind of the morning.

I tore through my closet, tossing clothes over my shoulder in my attempt to find something presentable to wear at the bakery. I managed to throw together an outfit that was suitable enough for the day, my fingers fumbling as I sent a quick text to my staff, apologizing for my tardiness and letting them know I was on my way.

As I hopped into my car, the memories of yesterday's outing with Jack flooded my mind. He had asked me out on a date, promising a day of fun and adventure on my next

Chapter Five 51

free day from the bakery. The thought brought a smile to my lips as I navigated the streets, excited for the prospect of something new and exciting.

Pulling up to the bakery, I couldn't shake the feeling that something was amiss. The girls behind the cashier counter exchanged furtive glances, and I couldn't help but feel a pang of worry.

"Oh, no," I said, approaching them. "Did Claudia put laundry detergent in the dishwasher again?"

"That was one time!" Claudia exclaimed. "*And,* it was an accident."

"No, it's not that," Isabella said. "Look what came for you!"

Claudia's eyes darted to the counter, and she reached under it to retrieve a stunning bouquet of lilies.

My gasp of surprise was involuntary as my fingers brushed over the delicate petals. They were exquisite, and I was taken aback by their beauty.

"Some very handsome, very muscular man brought these by this morning," Claudia said, a sly smile tugging at her lips.

The girls behind the counter erupted into excited whispers, their eyes fixed on me with a knowing gleam.

My heart raced with glee as I pulled out the envelope attached to the bouquet, my hands trembling slightly as I opened it.

The note inside was simple and sweet.

I can't wait to spend time with you.
Love, Jack

"Who's it from, Lydie?" Claudia asked.

Isabella squealed, her hands going over her mouth, trying to contain her excitement. "Is it from a boy?"

I chuckled, feeling my cheeks flush under their scrutiny.

"Yes, it's from... someone," I replied, trying to play it cool despite the flutter in my chest.

"Ugh!" Isabella groaned. "I wish a boy would send me flowers. That's so romantic. Are you going to see him again? Are you guys dating? I wish my mama would let me date! I'm almost seventeen. So unfair!"

At this point, two more members of my staff had joined the conversation, Lucy and Shelby, overhearing our conversation – and just as intrigued as the teenagers behind the register – they were waiting to hear my reply.

The problem was, I didn't know.

In the midst of the flurry of excitement and surprises that had unfolded in the last twenty-four hours, a subtle realization began to dawn on me. I was about to venture into the realm of dating.

It seemed almost unreal, a foreign concept that I hadn't seriously entertained for years. I didn't date. It wasn't as if I hadn't tried—a handful of awkward dates scattered through the years—but they had never amounted to anything substantial.

Now, here I was, caught up in the twister of emotions that Jack's return had stirred within me. Jack was no longer the boy I had known, the high school sweetheart who had stolen my heart. He was a man with experiences, growth, and a life I wasn't a part of.

The depth of my feelings for him was a revelation that I had yet to fully comprehend.

I loved the Jack I had once known, but could I love this new Jack? Did I even know him? There was an uncertainty that loomed, a question mark that hung in the air. *Do we pick up where we left? Or, do we create something new?*

My heart yearned for the chance to know him again, to discover the man that Jack Weston grew into.

But that journey involved dating, a concept that felt both thrilling and terrifying. The idea of opening myself up to the possibility of love again was a double-edged sword. Dating, to me, seemed like uncharted territory, a realm of unknowns that I hadn't fully reckoned with. The idea of getting to know Jack all over again, of navigating the complexities of his life and my own, felt like walking on a tightrope suspended above a sea of uncertainty.

I didn't like not knowing things.

Could we bridge the gap between our past and our present? Was it possible to create something meaningful out of the ashes of our old connection?

At that moment, I decided to take a leap of faith. I would embrace this new chapter with an open heart, ready to explore what might come next.

"We're going on a date later this week." I informed everyone.

I let the girls 'ooh' and 'aww' a moment longer before I pulled their focus back to working. The rest of the day went by pretty much unspectacularly, I kept busy with making desserts and talking with guests, but every once and awhile when a batch of cookies or a warm pie was passed over the counter, I would catch myself looking at the beautiful lilies that Jack had left for me.

"No, he did not!" Tori squealed, her hands and feet dancing in the air over the bed as she listened to me regale her and her mother about the lilies Jack gifted me. "Oh, that is *so* cute!"

The morning sun streamed through my windows, casting a warm glow over my living room as I busied myself setting out a spread of breakfast treats. Tori came over to watch Gus while I spent the day with Jack; because of his diabetes the cat needed insulin at a specific time, and I didn't want to miss that time and cause him any harm, so I asked Tori if she could look after him for a few hours. She had jumped at the chance, admitting that she wanted a break from motherhood for a short while, so she left Adam with his capable father and was in my house less than half an hour later.

Jack had suggested we visit the strawberry fields of a local winery, where we would indulge in a leisurely lunch and perhaps share a glass of wine or two before getting lost among the rows of sweet strawberries. It was a simple yet charming plan—one that conjured memories of my childhood, picking strawberries with my family and savoring their juicy sweetness.

Tori settled into a chair and flashed me a mischievous grin. "Don't worry, I've got this covered. And, you know, I've been wanting to hear more about this handsome Jack character."

Tori suggested that we video call her mother (my sister), Mira, who had always been my confidante and partner in crime. With Mira propped up on my vanity mirror through the video call, I began a mini fashion show, trying on different outfits to get their opinions.

When I came out in a knee-length black dress, Mira raised an eyebrow. "Lydie, you're stunning in anything you wear, but that dress makes you look like you're going to a funeral, not on a date. Next."

"Next," they said again when I put on an orange blouse.

Then, when I tried on a yellow one, Tori scrunched up her nose. "No, you look like a highlighter. Next."

"I don't even know if I have anything else!" I complained.

"Here," Tori said, getting up from the chair and walking into my closet. "Let me see... dang, Lydie, why do you have so much black?"

I shrugged. "It's the easiest thing to wear in the bakery."

"Hey, Mom! Do you know anything about this Jack guy?"

Mira happily confirmed, all too happy to reveal the contents of my earlier life. "Lydie was the captain of the cheerleading squad, and Jack was the captain of the football team. They were the perfect match, even back then. They were crowned king and queen of the prom, and the yearbook even voted them 'Most Likely To Marry.'"

Tori's eyes widened with amazement. "Really? 'Most Likely To Marry'? That's like a fairy tale!"

Mira nodded through the screen. "Oh, it was definitely stunning. They were inseparable, always together. And when they danced at the prom, it was like the world melted away and the rest of us were all just characters in Lydie's beautiful romance novel."

I rolled my eyes at the drama laced in her words.

Tori turned her gaze to me, a mischievous glint in her eyes. "Do you have any evidence of this epic prom night?"

"Actually, I think I might have something."

In the back of my closet, carefully tucked away, I still had the large box my prom dress came in. I retrieved the box and carefully lifted the lid, revealing a treasure trove of memories. More polaroids, a corsage, the program from the dance—all preserved as if time had stood still. And there, nestled among the keepsakes, were the crown and the tiara we had worn as Prom King and Queen, a reminder of a time when dreams were woven with a youthful innocence.

Tori's eyes shone with awe as she peeked into the box,

fingers brushing over the jewels of the tiara. "This is amazing, Aunt Lydie. You were royalty!"

I laughed. "I don't know about all of that. I'm pretty sure the tiara came from a department store clearance sale."

Tori, Mira, and I dug through the contents – me answering as many of their questions as I could. It wasn't until I lifted my old dress out of the box, dark purple and completely overruled by tulle. True to the seventies fashion, it had huge puffy sleeves that hung off of my shoulders and a full skirt that stopped just right at my calves.

Yet, even though the dress was beautiful, it was the old, worn pages folding into the folds of the dress that caught my attention. Gazing down at them now, I saw my own handwriting staring back at me.

These were pages from my own prayer book all those years ago.

I had scribbled it down on the day of my prom, a prayer whispered from the depths of my young heart. Even then, on the brink of our separation, I knew that our journey was changing, that we were growing in different directions. But the love we shared was a flame that I couldn't extinguish, even as reality pressed in.

So, with pen in hand and tears in my eyes, I poured out my hopes and fears onto those pages, asking God to grant me a simple request.

I prayed for his safety, his well-being as he ventured into the unknown, into the realm of overseas duty. My words were a plea, a plea for God's watchful eyes to be upon him, to shield him from harm. And intertwined with that plea was the whisper of my heart, the wish that someday, somehow, our paths might converge again.

As I read those words now, etched into the pages of the past, I was struck by the power of that young love, the faith that had guided my pen. The years had unfolded, carrying us along separate currents, but this prayer and my feelings remained.

I couldn't help but wonder if that prayer had played a role in leading us back to each other, decades later. I realized that sometimes, the desires of our hearts were answered in ways we couldn't even imagine.

When the time is right, my prayer said, *please, Lord, bring him back to me.*

Chapter Six

Jack

The morning of my date, I woke up with a smile on my face, the anticipation bubbling within me was almost palpable, and I felt like a teenager excited to see his crush.

I mean, technically, Lydie is my crush, and I wanted to make sure today of all days was particularly special for her.

However, after the incredible day spent uncovering the time capsule and asking her out on her next day off, fear immediately swooped in when I realized I had no idea where I wanted to take her. Nothing seemed good enough.

Not a movie. We wouldn't be able to talk, and I loved talking to her.

Dinner was a good option, but it wasn't particularly unique. I wanted her to be impressed.

Hiking? *Yeah, sure, Jack, make her work out on her day off. She'll really appreciate you for that.*

Dating was hard and I hadn't even truly started.

The day before our scheduled date, I paced around my living room, my mind racing as I tried to plan the perfect day. I wanted it to be something fun and memorable, something that would make Lydie smile and ease the day-to-day stress she must have running a business – even if it was only for just a few hours.

So, I mentally scrolled through the bits and pieces of information I had gathered all those years about her likes and dislikes.

And then it hit me – a memory she had shared with me once.

Strawberries.

She had told me about her parents taking her and her sister to strawberry fields when they were younger. They would spend the day picking strawberries and then when they went home, their mother would turn them into delicious desserts and treats. Lydie had spoken so fondly of those times of her childhood; I even remember the sadness in her voice when she said they stopped doing it as the girls got older.

How great would it be to be able to give her that experience again?

I knew there was a winery just outside of Beaufort that had strawberry fields open for picking. Without hesitation, I grabbed my phone and dialed their number. After booking a lunch reservation, a tour of the distillery, and time for strawberry picking, I hung up with a satisfied smile.

Accomplished, I sent a quick text to Lydie about the information of the date, telling her to wear comfortable shoes.

I'm so excited! was her reply.

On the day of the date, I told her I would pick her up

around eleven as our lunch reservation was at eleven-thirty, and it was at least a twenty-minute drive.

At eight-fifteen in the morning, I was too anxious to keep sleeping. So, after I made sure my mom was taken care of, I was back upstairs planning an outfit for a date that was two hours away.

As the hours ticked away, I found myself getting ready with a mix of anticipation and nervousness, feeling the exact same way I did the last time I met up with Lydie.

But this time, I was prepared.

Knowing I was going on a date, I had stopped by one of those men's department stores the other day, and picked out clothes I felt the best in. Beige slacks, brown belt, white button-down shirt I could easily roll up at the sleeves, and brown loafers. I even bought a nice-smelling hair gel that I could use to comb my hair back from my face.

This time when I looked in my mirror, I felt confident in my appearance.

"Wow!" Marcel said as I came downstairs. He and my mom were in the sunroom, watching more of that drama television my mother loved so much. "Now, that is definitely a date outfit."

"You look so handsome, sweetie!" My mom cooed. "Where's my camera? Marcel, dear, do you know where my phone is?"

"Mom," I groaned in that way only sons do with their mothers, "I'm fifty-two years old. Not twelve."

She looked at me with a stern expression. "I don't care if you're seventy, young man." Marcel handed her her phone. "You're never too old to get your picture taken. Now, smile. Say cheese."

"Cheese," I grumbled out, smiling at the same time the flash on her phone went off.

Chapter Six 61

"Perfect, now, have a fun time! Don't forget, I raised you to be a gentleman, so you better act like one!"

Right on schedule, I walked across the street to Lydie's house. I knocked on the door, and when she opened it, I was floored by her beauty.

As Lydie opened the door, my breath caught in my throat. She stood before me, radiating a beauty that had me feeling momentarily self-conscious.

This gorgeous woman is choosing to spend the day with me?

She wore a pale pink t-shirt that was tucked into a pair of ankle-length denim jeans. The outfit exuded a casual yet stylish charm, and her choice of white sandals and a sun hat with a white ribbon added to the overall charm. Her long, dark hair cascaded down her shoulders, adorned with soft, lightweight curls.

The sight of her took my breath away, and for a moment, words failed me. But as she smiled warmly and greeted me, I found my voice again. "Lydie, you look absolutely stunning."

Her cheeks flushed with a touch of embarrassment, and she waved off the compliment. "Oh, Jack, stop it. You're too kind."

But the truth was, her beauty was undeniable, and it was more than just her appearance – it was the way her smile reached her eyes, the way she carried herself with a blend of confidence and humility.

I was the luckiest guy on the earth.

The twenty-minute drive to the winery seemed to pass quickly as we chatted effortlessly, the ease of our conversation only confirming how comfortable I was in her presence.

When the song Lydie liked started to play on the radio,

she glanced at me with a hopeful smile. "Mind if we turn it up a bit?"

"Of course not," I replied, reaching for the knob without hesitation. Her happiness was infectious, and I was more than willing to indulge her in this small pleasure.

As the music filled the car, her face lit up, and she couldn't help but start dancing and singing along. Her voice was off-key, and her dance moves were more enthusiastic than coordinated, but watching her let loose and enjoy herself was a sight to behold. The way her laughter mingled with the music, the carefree spirit she exuded – it was nothing short of adorable.

As I turned onto the gravel road leading to the winery, my anticipation grew with every passing second.

"Ohh!" Lydie gasped, excited.

Finally, after only driving up a short driveway the winery emerged into view, a harmonious blend of rustic charm and refined elegance. The main building exuded a timeless appeal, with its weathered wooden exterior and gracefully arched windows.

A tasteful sign proudly announced the winery's restaurant and where to go for information on tours or fruit picking, and I parked the car in a spot dedicated for visitors.

Getting out of the vehicle, Lydie and I were entranced with the heady aroma of ripe strawberries mingled with the faint hint of fermentation from the nearby winery, creating a unique olfactory experience that hinted at the pleasures to come.

Walking into the winery's welcoming atmosphere, we were greeted by a host who showed us to our reserved table. As we followed the host to our seats, I was immediately struck by the seamless blend of casual comfort and understated sophistication. The interior exuded a sense of refined rusticity, with a contemporary twist that elevated the atmosphere. Polished wooden floors extended beneath my feet, while exposed beams crossed over the ceiling, evoking a cozy and open ambiance.

The walls held tasteful artwork that celebrated the winemaking process, showcasing the intricate details of vineyards, strawberry clusters, and the subtle play of sunlight filtering through the leaves. Soft, muted colors dominated the palette, creating an inviting space that was both relaxed and elegant.

The tables were dressed in crisp white linens, complemented by simple yet stylish cutlery and glassware. Each setting exuded thoughtfulness, embodying the attention to detail that defined the establishment.

Large windows framed the panoramic view of the surrounding vineyards, allowing natural light to flood the space. The sight of rows upon rows of strawberry vines stretching into the distance captivated me.

"Here is your table."

"Thank you," I told the host as she handed us our menus and the wine list.

"Your server will be right with you."

We didn't have to wait long, and when the server greeted us, I tried to listen intently to the speech he gave us about the chef's specials and all of the different wines listed on the menu, but I was failing miserably. I didn't normally drink wine. Give me an ice-cold beer on a hot summer's day, but wine? It was fine, but I didn't go out of my way for it, so when the server started talking about "finishes" and the "notes" of a good wine, I was completely lost.

"Is there a bottle I could get you guys to start you off with?"

"Er," I stumbled to think, looking down at the extensive

wine list before me. I didn't want to order something for the both of us and then be responsible for drinking a wine that neither of us liked.

Thankfully, the server came to my rescue. "We do have wine flights. You get a choice of six sample pours of different wines, all made from the strawberries in our fields, to taste. We like to suggest pairing the flight with our signature charcuterie board to sample with, as the board is specifically curated to compliment the taste of each wine."

"That sounds great, actually." I chose three wines from the list that looked good, and Lydie chose the other three.

As we waited for our wines to arrive along with the appetizer, Lydie inquired about my mother's well-being.

I couldn't help but smile at her genuine concern. "She's hanging in there," I replied, my tone reflecting a mix of gratitude and a touch of weariness. "The hospice care can be challenging at times, but I wouldn't trade this time with her for anything. Plus, it helps a lot to have Marcel helping as much as he does.

Lydie's eyes held a warmth that spoke volumes of her empathy. "You're doing such a wonderful thing, Jack. Your mother is lucky to have you by her side."

The genuine sincerity in her words touched me, and I nodded appreciatively. "Thank you, Lydie."

"I should stop by sometime, I used to bring her a pecan pie from the bakery all of the time. I haven't in a while because I've been so busy, but I should make an effort."

My heart swelled with gratitude for her kind gesture. "That would mean a lot to both of us," I said. "My mother always loved your pies."

First out of the kitchen was the charcuterie board,

adorned with many different cheeses, fruits, meat, and bread. The wine flights followed suit, each glass holding a promise of unique flavors and experiences.

One particular wine captured our attention, a perfect blend of sweetness and boldness that resonated with both of our palates. We exchanged smiles as we decided on this shared choice, and our glasses were soon filled with its rich contents.

The conversation flowed seamlessly as we sipped the wine, the words weaving between sips and laughter.

As the anticipation of lunch grew, we placed our orders. My choice was a garden panini with prosciutto. Lydie, on the other hand, opted for the lunch special – charbroiled salmon nestled in a delicate pasta bathed in lemon and herb butter sauce.

When the food arrived, the conversation paused as our senses were captivated by the visual and aromatic delights before us. As I took my first bite of the panini, I couldn't help but express my delight, prompting Lydie's curiosity.

"Is it really that good?" she asked, a playful glint in her eyes.

I nodded enthusiastically, realizing that I had an opportunity to share the experience with her. "You should try it," I suggested, my fork poised with a morsel of the panini.

Without thinking too much of it, I extended my arm across the table, offering her a bite. The act itself felt very intimate, and I worried it was too forward of me, yet as she leaned forward to accept the morsel, an unexpected surge of happiness tingled through our connection. Her lips closed around the fork, and my heart skipped a beat as I watched her savor the bite.

"Mmm," she groaned, pleased. "That is good!"

. . .

Her subsequent offer to share a part of her salmon was too good of an offer to pass up, and I, too, leaned in to take a bite of her food. Between bites, we would exchange appreciative glances and nods of agreement.

As we finished our lunch, both Lydie and I were completely satisfied and fueled for the rest of the day. I paid the server, leaving him a generous tip for his help and expertise.

Leaving the restaurant, the sun bathed the winery's grounds in a warm afternoon glow. Following the signs that pointed the way, Lydie and I made our way to the designated area for the tour. As we approached one of the barn-like buildings, a small group of people had already gathered. It was then that I realized the tours were conducted in groups, a fact I had momentarily overlooked when making the reservations. But as Lydie and I joined the line, it became apparent that this communal experience could be just as enjoyable, if not more so.

We didn't have to wait long before the tour commenced.

Our guide led us into the heart of the distillery, where the air carried a cluster of aromas – the unmistakable scent of aging oak, the lingering essence of strawberries, and the subtle notes of fermentation.

As we moved among the barrels, each one holding the promise of a unique vintage, Lydie's captivated expression mirrored my own fascination.

Halfway through the tour, as we navigated our way through the barrel-lined pathways, I mustered the courage to make a move I had been contemplating. I reached for Lydie's hand.

Our fingers intertwined naturally as if they were destined to fit together.

I was astounded by the immediate comfort that settled

between us. Her hand felt delicate yet strong, and I couldn't help but marvel at the way her presence made me feel – at ease and exhilarated all at once.

With every step we took, the clinking of barrels and the rhythmic narration of the guide faded into the background. The tour continued, but my focus was firmly fixed on the warmth of Lydie's hand in mine.

The sensation of Lydie's fingers entwined with mine was both exhilarating and comforting.

It was a simple gesture, yet it held a weight of significance that was impossible to ignore. As the guide's words washed over us, I found myself struggling to articulate just how incredible it felt to hold onto her once again.

The last time I had held her hand was more than three decades ago, in a different time and place. Yet, this touch felt new, almost unfamiliar in its intensity. It was as if the years had peeled away, leaving us with the raw, unfiltered connection that had been there all along.

As we moved through the distillery, the past and present seemed to blur together. We weren't the young couple we once were, but the emotions I felt for Lydie were just as potent. The sensations, the butterflies in my stomach, the sense of being drawn to her – they were all eerily reminiscent of the feelings I had experienced as a young man.

In those moments, I could almost transport myself back in time, to a time when life was simpler, and love was a promise shared between two hearts.

It struck me that love, in its purest form, could be both timeless and ageless.

As adults, we have faced life's challenges, taken separate paths, and grown in ways we could never have predicted. Yet, the core of our connection remained steadfast, as if it had been waiting for the right moment to rekindle.

With every step we took, every glance we exchanged, I found myself falling deeper into the emotions that had defined our past. The years melted away, leaving only the palpable sense of affection that had endured the test of time.

As the tour concluded and we stepped back into the sunlight, I held onto Lydie's hand a little tighter.

With each shared moment, the touch of her hand, and every glimpse into her eyes, I felt a familiar warmth spreading through my heart. It was as if the years had fallen away, and I was falling in love with Lydie all over again, and this time, it felt like it was all a part of God's plan.

Chapter Seven

Lydie

As Jack and I wandered through the distillery, the air rich with the heady scent of aging spirits, I couldn't help but feel giddy. His fingers found mine naturally, intertwining with a familiarity that both surprised and delighted me. Decades had separated us, and yet in this moment, holding his hand felt like the most natural thing in the world.

The tour had taken us through the intricate process of distilling, a dance of science and craftsmanship that left me fascinated. I was enthralled by the passion and dedication that went into creating these spirits. I was even happier with the presence of Jack by my side.

The prayer page I had stumbled upon that morning—resonated with me in a way I couldn't fully explain. The words I had penned, the plea for Jack's safety and the wish for our paths to converge again, felt like echoes of my heart's desires.

Did Jesus truly bring Jack back into my life? Was this a sign that the time was finally right, that the love I had tucked away within me had found its way back to the surface?

Walking together through the tour, I realized that my feelings for Jack had never truly faded. Instead, they had been carefully folded and stored in the recesses of my heart, as if protected by a mental block I had constructed over the years. It wasn't that I had gotten over him—it was more that I had closed off that part of myself, choosing to focus on my bakery, my career, and the life I had built.

And yet, here he was, standing by my side with his vibrant smile and the same magnetic energy that had drawn me to him in the first place. But as I looked into his eyes, I saw glimpses of the Jack I had known, the boy who also held my hand on our very first date together almost thirty-five years ago.

Jack was great, there was no denying that. His kindness, his sense of humor, his zest for life—it all shone through, creating a warmth that enveloped me. As we continued walking, the evening breeze tangling with our hair, I found myself pondering the possibility of a future together.

As we neared the end of the tour, our guide introduced us to a section of the distillery that piqued my curiosity—where they stored their cooking wines. The idea was intriguing, and as our guide handed around a plate of delicate cookies, she explained that while the cookies themselves were ordinary sugar cookies, the icing and the candied strawberry on top were created using the strawberries from the field.

My taste buds tingled as my senses were immediately greeted with an explosion of flavor. The wine-infused elements elevated the simple cookie into a symphony of taste.

I couldn't help but express my delight. "Oh, this is incredible!"

Jack nodded in agreement, a smile playing at the corners of his lips. "It's like a burst of summer in every bite."

As we savored the treats, an elderly woman approached us. "I couldn't help but overhear your praise for our wine-infused cookies. I'm thrilled that you enjoyed them. My name is Suzannah, my husband and I own this winery."

I was taken aback only for a moment that we were meeting one of the owners. "Oh my, it's such an honor to meet you. Your wine is amazing."

Her smile widened. "The honor is mine. Lydie Dawson, is it? I read about your bakery in *Southern Treats and Charm*. It's not often we have someone with your expertise and passion visit us. If it's not too forward of me to ask, I'd love to know your thoughts on using our wines in your baking."

I was both flattered and humbled by her words. To have someone appreciate my work and extend such an invitation was beyond anything I had expected. The idea of incorporating their unique wines into my bakery creations intrigued me, and I found myself genuinely excited at the prospect.

"That sounds like an incredible opportunity," I replied, my heart racing with appreciation and enthusiasm. "I've always believed in exploring new avenues to create flavors that delight the senses. Using your wines to infuse that magic into my baked goods could be a wonderful experiment."

The owner's eyes sparkled with approval. "I'm thrilled to

hear that. I'll have a case of our most popular wines brought to the front of the restaurant. You can pick it up before you leave here."

As Suzannah left us to introduce herself to the other guests, Jack gently nudged me in the stomach to get my attention. "Look at you, boss lady!" He beamed.

"I know!" I practically squealed. "She knows who I am!"

Jack laughed. "You know, I should get your autograph, so I can say I knew you before you were super famous."

"Okay, but it'll cost you twenty dollars. I'm a working artist."

As we walked out of the distillery, the sun greeted us with its gentle warmth. The excitement in the air was thick as the staff handed each of us a straw basket.

I rummaged through my purse, retrieving a bottle of sunscreen, a vital companion for a day spent under the sun. With a smile, I offered some to Jack, but my laughter bubbled forth when I saw the comically oversized glob of sunscreen he had smeared onto his cheek.

"You seem to have embraced the sunscreen application with a bit too much enthusiasm," I teased, my voice laced with amusement.

Jack chuckled, his cheeks turning slightly pink. "Seems like I got a bit carried away there."

"Here, let me help you."

As my fingertip brushed against his skin, a jolt of electricity radiated through me. I watched as Jack's eyes met mine, and for a fleeting moment, the world around us seemed to fade, leaving only the two of us in a bubble of shared connection.

The sensation of his skin beneath my touch was both familiar and new, a paradox that left me yearning for more. But before I could lose myself completely, I focused on the task at hand, gently rubbing the sunscreen into his skin.

My fingers moved with a tenderness that mirrored the feelings I had long held for him.

With the sunscreen successfully applied and any lingering awkwardness dissipated with shared laughter, we ventured into the sunlit fields. The rows of strawberry plants stretched before us like a vibrant sea of red and green, a feast for the eyes, and a promise of sweet treasures waiting to be plucked.

As we moved through the fields, my heart swelled with a sense of nostalgia. Picking strawberries had been a cherished activity in my childhood, a tradition that held a special place in my heart. Now, sharing this experience with Jack, it felt like I was weaving the threads of my past into the present, blending memories with newfound moments.

With care and precision, we selected the ripest, juiciest strawberries we could find. When our baskets were filled with the spoils of our labor, we headed back toward the shaded areas, where the cool breeze danced through the leaves of the trees.

Jack bought us a couple of cold waters from the gift shop, and we settled down beneath the shelter of a sprawling tree. With the strawberry-scented air surrounding us, we opened our baskets and began to nibble on our sweet rewards.

The strawberries burst with flavor, each bite a symphony of taste that awakened my senses. As I glanced at Jack, his lips smeared with the deep red hue of the fruit, a feeling of contentment settled over me.

I couldn't help but marvel at the serendipity of it all. The distillery tour had led us here, where strawberries and shared laughter seemed to bridge the gap between the past and the present.

As we finished the last strawberries and watched the world around us, I felt a sense of gratitude well up within me. This day, this date with Jack, was a gift—a reminder that sometimes, the most beautiful moments could be found in the simplest of experiences and that the journey of love, no matter how complex, could be as sweet and satisfying as the ripest strawberry on a summer's day.

I turned to Jack, unable to resist the urge to study his features, his every detail etching itself into my memory.

His hair combed back in an effortlessly handsome manner, and the way he had rolled his sleeves up over his elbows revealed forearms that were both strong and inviting. The wrinkles that time had painted onto his face seemed to add character to the man he had become, and yet, underneath it all, I still saw the boy I had once loved so deeply.

Jack's voice broke through my reverie, drawing me back to the present. "Lydie, I've had an amazing day with you."

A smile tugged at my lips as my heart swelled with happiness. "Jack, thank you for this wonderful date. It's been such a memorable day—one I'll treasure for years to come."

"That's exactly what I wanted. To create a day you'll always remember."

His words hung in the air, lingering like a promise. And then, as if drawn by an invisible force, he leaned in.

My heart raced, a mixture of anticipation and nerves swirling within me. I closed my eyes.

But as his face drew closer, I felt a soft pressure against

my cheek, a gentle kiss that left my skin tingling. My heart skipped a beat as the reality of the moment settled in—he had kissed my cheek, not my lips. My eyes snapped open and I almost giggled at my own folly.

As he pulled away slightly, our eyes met, and I saw a hint of something in his gaze—affection. I didn't want to overanalyze it; I wanted to revel in the magic of the present.

So, with a smile that held a touch of shyness, I shifted on the bench, leaning my head against his shoulder. It was a movement that felt natural as if we were picking up a thread of intimacy that had been woven long ago.

His arm encircled me, drawing me close in a way that felt both protective and comforting. My heart thrummed with a sense of belonging, a feeling that had eluded me for years. We sat there, side by side, the world around us fading into the background as I nestled against him, feeling his warmth and his presence enveloping me.

As I listened to the rhythm of his breathing, I realized that sometimes, the most profound moments were found in the simplest of gestures—the brush of lips against skin, hand holding, cuddling on a public bench, it was also so innocent but sweet. I allowed myself to embrace the possibility that the love I had tucked away, the love that had endured the test of time, was finding its way back to the surface.

I closed my eyes and allowed myself to savor the sensation—the feeling of being close to him, the memory of his kiss against my cheek, and the promise of a future that held the potential for a love that was as enduring as the years that had passed.

The evening had taken on a golden hue as Jack escorted me to my front door, a true gentleman in every sense. My cheeks ached from the genuine smiles that had graced my lips throughout the day. It had been a day of rediscovering, rekindling, and forging new memories with a person who had once held the key to my heart.

"Tori!" I called out as soon as I opened the door. "I'm home."

"Great!" Her voice echoed from somewhere within the house. "Gus missed you!"

In response to her words, I heard a contented "meow" from my feline friend.

"That cat really does love you," Jack remarked.

I chuckled affectionately. "Oh, I love him, too. I'm definitely getting my own cat."

I turned back to face Jack and found him standing much closer than I had expected. His proximity was almost intoxicating, and I couldn't help but be drawn into the magnetic pull that always happened when I was with him.

Our faces were mere inches apart, and I felt my heart quicken as Jack's eyes shifted from mine to my lips. It was a moment charged with a palpable tension; the anticipation of another kiss lept in my mind.

"Hey, Lydie—" Tori's voice cut through the air, breaking the spell just as it threatened to deepen. Her realization that she had interrupted something hung in the atmosphere, but she managed a nervous smile before retreating back around the corner and disappearing from view.

Instead of frustration, Jack and I shared a soft, knowing giggle, a shared understanding that sometimes life had its own timing and sense of humor.

As the moment settled, Jack's voice broke the silence. "I wanted to ask if you'd like to come over sometime this week for dinner. My mom has been asking about you."

The offer warmed my heart, and my smile deepened. My cheeks throbbed from the day's laughter, but the prospect of spending more time with Jack and his family filled me with happiness. "I would love that, Jack," I replied, my voice filled with genuine enthusiasm.

With a final exchange of smiles, Jack bid me goodnight. As I watched him walk away, my heart swelled with gratitude to the Lord above. Jack was officially back in my life.

Now safe, Tori popped her head out from the living room. "I am so sorry."

I gave her a hug. "It's okay. Everything has its timing. How was Gus?"

Tori recounted the evening she spent with Gus, and how even though she loved Adam, it felt nice to get out of the house for a bit. She gave me another hug before also leaving, ready to return to her favorite job as a mother. I closed the door behind her, and because I had so much energy from the exciting night that I could finally release without any prying eyes, I squealed out and did a little dance.

Once that was out of my system, I grabbed my phone from my back pocket and sent a quick text message.

Are you up? I have news!

My sister's response was almost immediate.

Call me now. I have to know everything!

With a smile tugging at my lips, I dialed Mira's number.

"Hey, it's me," I greeted, my voice bubbling with excitement.

"Lydie! How did it go? Tell me everything!" Mira's enthusiasm mirrored my own.

I settled onto the couch, Gus curling up beside me, and began recounting the day's events—the distillery tour, the strawberry picking, and the two almost-kisses that had left me feeling both exhilarated and a little breathless. Mira listened intently, and I could almost see the delighted grin on her face.

"Oh my goodness, Lydie! That's incredible! It sounds like you had the perfect date!" Mira's voice brimmed with excitement.

I couldn't help but laugh, my heart feeling light and joyous. "It really was, Mira. Jack is amazing, and spending the day with him felt like a dream."

"Oh, I'm so jealous. Tell me more!"

We continued to talk, sharing stories, laughter, and a deep bond that only sisters could understand. As my yawn interrupted our conversation, I decided to retreat to my room, Gus trailing behind me.

Dressed in my comfortable pajamas, I collapsed onto my bed with a contented sigh. Lying on my stomach, I let my feet kick back and forth in the air, a playful gesture that reflected the giddiness I felt inside. It was as if I had been transported back to my teenage years, the rush of emotions making me feel like a schoolgirl with a crush.

As I played with the loose stitching on my comforter, my thoughts drifted to a memory from long ago—the late-night talk Mira and I had shared when I was sixteen and had just gone out on a date with Jack for the first time. The memories of that night were etched into my heart, and I couldn't help but smile at the parallels between then and now.

With a chuckle, I dialed back into the phone call with Mira, sharing every detail, including what I felt with the near-kisses.

"Lydie, this is incredible! I'm so happy for you!"

"Thanks, Mira. I can't believe how everything unfolded today. It's like fate brought us back together."

Mira's voice softened with affection. "You deserve all the happiness in the world, little sis. I'm so glad Jack is back in your life."

The warmth of her words spread through me, a reminder of the unwavering support and love that Mira had always provided. We continued to chat, our conversation flowing effortlessly, as if time hadn't separated us at all.

As I finally hung up the phone, a sense of contentment settled over me. I rolled over onto my back, staring up at the ceiling, my heart full of hope, excitement, and the deep comfort of knowing that I had a sister who was there to share in my joys and triumphs.

With Gus purring beside me, I closed my eyes, savoring the happiness that surrounded me. And as I drifted off to sleep, I carried the memory of laughter, the feeling of Jack's near-kisses, and the warmth of Mira's words.

Chapter Eight

Jack

Why did I think I could do this?

I had invited Lydie over for dinner, eager to create a special meal for her. But there was a small detail I had overlooked in my eagerness to impress her – my culinary skills were practically non-existent.

Years of military service had conditioned me to rely on packaged rations and the occasional takeout, leaving me unacquainted with the kitchen's nuances. I was just too busy and uninspired to take up any real cooking skills.

Determined to create a memorable dish, I had settled on chicken parmigiana and garlic bread – Lydie's favorite. Armed with a printed recipe and God's good faith, I navigated the grocery store and left with everything I needed for the perfect date. I thought, as long as I had ingredients, everything else would be easy, right?

Wrong.

Chapter Eight

The evening arrived, and the kitchen became my battleground. As I prepped the ingredients, I tried to follow the recipe step by step, attempting to mimic the rhythm of a seasoned chef.

If that Chef were Chef Boyardee.

As soon as I pulled out the chicken and saw how undercooked it was, its exterior was a far cry from the crispy golden perfection I had envisioned. The garlic bread, which I had innocently left under the broiler for "just a minute," had taken on an unappetizing shade of black. And then there were the noodles. Somehow, in my attempts to multitask, the pasta had transformed into a massive clump, stubbornly adhering to the bottom of the pot.

It was a culinary catastrophe of epic proportions, and I felt my hopes of impressing Lydie slipping through my fingers like sand.

It didn't help when my mother wheeled herself into the kitchen, her neck stretching so that she could see into the pot.

"I don't think it's supposed to look like that," she said.

My lips quirked in an unamused smirk. "You think? Any ideas on what to do?"

"Yeah," she scrunched her nose in disgust when she sniffed the charred garlic bread, "throw it out."

"Ugh, Lydie's going to be here any second!"

The doorbell rang, signaling Lydie's arrival, and a wave of panic surged within me.

"Crap!"

"Language, young man," my mom scolded. "Just breathe. We can figure something out. Now, go. Don't make your date wait outside."

Shoulders slumped and my mood soured, I put down the dish towel I was holding and left the kitchen.

Opening the front door, my mood was instantly lifted by the sight of Lydie's beauty. She stood before me, radiant and enchanting, wearing a dark purple dress that hugged her curves gracefully. Ruffled sleeves stopped just above her elbows, adding a touch of whimsy. The dress boasted a v-neck neckline, which drew my gaze to the delicate gold chain around her neck, supporting a locket— a locket I had gifted her for her seventeenth birthday.

Her long, dark hair cascaded in loose curls around her shoulders, and while I had never been one to pay much attention to makeup, I couldn't deny that Lydie looked absolutely stunning with every delicate touch. A hint of lipgloss accentuated her smile, and mascara drew attention to her mesmerizing blue eyes.

"Hi." She smiled at me.

"Hi," I said back, never taking my eyes off of her.

In her arms, she cradled a freshly baked pecan pie. The aroma of the pie wafted through the air, filling the space with a comforting, sweet scent that instantly made my mouth water.

I stepped aside to allow her entry, taking in the sight of her as she kicked off her shoes at the doorway— always remembering my mom's house rule.

As she breathed in the air, her brows furrowed slightly, and she turned to me with a playful curiosity. "Is something burning, Jack?"

A flush of embarrassment crept over me, and I couldn't help but chuckle ruefully. "You could say that. I had a bit of a mishap in the kitchen. I ruined dinner."

Lydie's laughter, light and melodious, danced through the room like a gentle breeze.

"Jack," she said, her voice warm and reassuring,

"everyone has their strengths... You're just lucky that mine is cooking."

With a grin, she handed me the pecan pie and began to make her way toward the kitchen. As I followed her, I couldn't help but feel a profound sense of gratitude. Despite my culinary shortcomings, Lydie's presence had a way of turning even the most chaotic of situations into moments of mirth.

"Hi, Viv!" she greeted my mom kindly. "It's so nice to see you. I brought a pie."

"Oh, dear, you're so sweet. I can't wait to try it."

Lydie walked around the kitchen island, surveying the mess and culinary wreckage.

"If you want to help me with the dishes," she looked at me, "I can make us a great meal."

I frowned. "I don't want to make you cook for us. I asked you on this date, it would be rude. We can just order pizza."

Lydie was already shaking her head before I even finished my sentence. "Nah, that won't do. Plus," she winked at me, "now, I want chicken parm."

Knowing better than to argue with her, I cleaned up as much of my mess as I could and cleaned the dishes. To stave off their hunger while I worked, Lydie cut her and my mom a small slice of her pie.

"We have vanilla bean ice cream in the freezer," my mom informed Lydie.

"Oh, that would be perfect."

I pouted. "What about my slice?"

"You get a piece when the kitchen is cleaned."

"Bossy," I teased her.

As soon as the last pan was clean and drying, Lydie cut me a slice of the pie and loaded me up with some ice cream while she replaced me at the island. Thankfully, I hadn't measured the amount of ingredients I would need for this recipe, so I had bought extras for everything.

As Lydie bustled around the kitchen, effortlessly preparing the ingredients for dinner, I couldn't help but feel a profound sense of appreciation for her. Instead of being upset or disappointed, she had taken charge and saved the day, fixing what I had failed to achieve.

My mother and I watched Lydie as she moved around the kitchen. The gentle sway of her hips, the way she expertly chopped vegetables, and the way she checked on the bubbling pots on the stove – it all spoke years of expertise. I couldn't help but admire her, not just for her cooking skills, but for her resilience and her willingness to step in and help without a second thought.

As my mom and I chatted with Lydie, the atmosphere felt light and comfortable. Lydie's genuine interest in my mom's well-being was evident as she asked about her health. My mom, always honest and forthright, shared her struggles with being confined to a wheelchair, one of the consequences of her last stroke and heart failure diagnosis.

"It's not easy," she said, sadly. "I miss my garden. I miss being able to move on my own."

My mother had always been an active person, a woman of purposefulness, who embraced each day with vigor. But since her last stroke, her body had become a prison, too weak to carry her through her usual activities for long periods.

I reached out and took her hand. "I'll help you more. I can carry you to the garden if I have to."

My mother giggled, patting my hand. "Thank you, Jack, but it's okay. This old body just can't do as much as it used to, and I have to respect that. I'm not going anywhere, yet. God still has plans for this ol' lady."

We all laughed and agreed with her.

As the enticing aroma of the chicken parmigiana began to fill the kitchen, our appetites were thoroughly whetted, and conversation became stilted as we waited for it to be done. My mom and I exchanged eager glances; it'd been a while since we had a meal that didn't come from a prepackaged box.

The table was set with care, the soft glow of candlelight dancing on the silverware and plates as I lit the candles.

"Not those," my mom said to me as I pulled a couple of plastic cups from the cabinet. "Get the crystal."

I raised my eyebrow. "Whoa, the crystal? Is it someone's birthday?"

Mom gave me a look that said she didn't appreciate my jesting. "Jack Lawrence Weston, don't tease your mother. It is a special night because we have a beautiful young woman with us, and we should try and impress her. Otherwise, who knows if she'll want to come back."

Lydie blushed at her compliment.

Great, my mom is better at flirting with my date than I am.

I grabbed the crystal glasses from the dutch cabinet in the dining room and placed them around our dishes. As Lydie plated the chicken parmigiana with a touch of finesse, arranging it with a garnish of fresh herbs that added a burst of color, I grabbed a few cans of Coke from the fridge and poured them over ice in each of the cups.

When I looked up, Lydie was smiling.

"What?" I asked her.

"Thank you for helping tonight."

Shocked, I said, "*Thank me?* I should be thanking you! You saved my butt tonight."

"Yes, but you cleaned the dishes and set the table. A chef always needs help in the kitchen."

I chuckled. "I will always be willing to help you. Whenever you need it."

I meant it. There was nothing she couldn't ask me that I wouldn't do for her.

We all sat around the dining table, and Mom elected to say Grace.

"Thank you, Lord," she started, our hands joined together and our eyes closed to focus on the graceful words she spoke. "Thank you for this food we are about to receive — lovingly prepared by the most wonderful woman, Lydie. Thank you, for allowing us to be here tonight, and thank you, Lord, for guiding us with nothing but love and support. In Your precious name, Jesus, we pray, Amen."

We didn't wait a second more before digging in.

As soon as the first bite hit my tongue, the flavors exploded on my palate, and I inwardly groaned in happiness. The chicken was tender, the tomato sauce rich, and the melted cheese perfectly gooey.

Beside me, my mother's eyes sparkled with a light that had been missing for a while. "Lydie, dear, this is absolutely amazing."

"Thank you, Viv."

"She's not wrong." I also complimented. "I feel like I never want to eat anything else but this."

Lydie chuckled. "Well, the chicken does offer a lot of protein."

As we indulged in our meal, we shared stories and memories, each of us opening up and connecting in ways that felt both comfortable and heartwarming.

Amid the exchange of stories, my mother chimed in with a memory from the past.

She recalled my nervousness before my first date with Lydie all those years ago. She recounted how I had changed my clothes countless times that day, my anxiety evident to everyone around me. It was true; that first date had me more flustered than I cared to admit.

"I was sixteen!" I defended myself as Lydie laughed at Mom's story. "I was so scared! Plus, your father was chaperoning, and I just wanted him to like me."

"He always liked you!" Lydie promised.

"Yeah, but before I was just the kid across the street. After that, I was your boyfriend. Trust me, it was terrifying."

The conversation continued and Mom shared a touching sentiment that left a profound impact on both Lydie and me.

"I knew it was love," she told us both, "the way you two looked at each other— it was how I used to look at your father."

She recounted her own love story, how she had met my father when she was just seventeen, and the seventy years they had spent together had been filled with challenges and rewards alike.

Then, her face became contemplative, and she turned to look at a frame hanging on the wall. It was a picture of her and my dad, Steve, at mom's fiftieth birthday.

"He's been gone almost ten years, now." She sighed. "I miss him every day, but I know he's with God now, and that's the best thing any of us could hope for."

Suddenly, my face fell. I couldn't help but be overwhelmed by a wave of emotions and memories. My mother's story of love had been heartwarming, but as she talked about Dad's funeral, it stirred something deeper within me—a painful regret that had remained buried for far too long.

It was a regret that had haunted me for years, a memory I could never erase or amend. I had found out about my dad's passing when I was stationed in Iraq. The news had shattered my world and left me feeling utterly helpless. My father was gone, and I was half a world away, unable to be there for his final moments or attend his funeral.

I had desperately tried to secure leave, but when you're on active duty, leave isn't always guaranteed and my request was denied, and I wasn't there for his funeral to pay my respects. The anger, frustration, and despair I had felt during that time were indescribable.

My father had been a pillar of strength, a source of unwavering love and support throughout my life. His values of hard work, compassion, and selflessness had shaped me into the person I had become. Losing him was a blow that left a void in my heart, one that could not be easily refilled.

Yet, just as darkness threatened to consume me for the rest of the night, Lydie's touch beneath the table brought me back to the present moment. Her hand found mine, and her gentle squeeze was like a lifeline, pulling me out of the depths of my grief and regret.

"Your husband's service was lovely," she told my mom across the table. "He was loved by many and cherished the most by his family." She looked directly at me. "He knew that."

Wet warmth stung my eyes as I listened to the words Lydie said. *He knew he was loved.*

As we continued to share stories and laughter, I held Lydie's hand beneath the table, grateful for the light she had brought into my life. In that moment, I understood that while I could never change the past, I could shape the future.

And, I wanted Lydie to be a part of it.

In that moment, as the candlelight flickered and the stories flowed, it was as if the past, present, and future converged. The echoes of young love and the promise of new beginnings mingled in the air, creating an atmosphere that was both sentimental and hopeful.

The night had grown late, and my mother was tired from all the excitement. I helped her to her room, ensuring she was comfortable and settled in her bed. She looked up at me with a contented smile.

"I had such a great night tonight, Jack. Thank you for inviting Lydie over," she told me.

That smile was worth more to me than anything else in the world, and it filled my heart with joy. I kissed her on the forehead. "I'm glad, Mom. Now, get some sleep."

After leaving my mother's room, I rejoined Lydie in the living room. We decided to take a leisurely walk to the dock at the back of her house.

I grabbed a pitcher of my mother's famous blueberry lemonade and a couple of cups. The South Carolina night air was warm and pleasant, and I figured we might get thirsty.

As we strolled together, I couldn't help but express my gratitude. "Thank you for tonight," I said sincerely. "You've made this evening so enjoyable. Every time I'm with you, I just feel happy and comfortable."

Lydie smiled at me, her eyes reflecting the moonlight.

We reached the dock and sat down side by side, our feet

dangling in the cool lake water. We held hands, our fingers intertwining naturally. The sound of crickets and the gentle lapping of the water against the shore provided a soothing backdrop to our conversation.

It was there that I opened up further about my father.

"I mostly worried about my mom," I admitted. "She had to go through losing my dad alone."

Lydie's expression softened with understanding. "I'm so sorry, Jack. I can't even imagine how hard it was for you to not be there." Then, she caught my gaze and held it while she said, "But she's a strong woman, and she had the support of the whole town. They cared for her during that time. She wasn't alone."

Her hand squeezed mine reassuringly. "Your mom is an incredible woman, just like you. She raised a wonderful son."

I turned to her, my heart feeling strangely full. "Lydie, you're absolutely wonderful. I can't believe I survived this long without you. I— don't think I can do it again."

Our eyes locked, and in that moment, the unspoken words between us hung in the air. I leaned in, and she met me halfway. Our lips met in a soft, tender kiss.

It was a kiss filled with the promise of what could be, a kiss that spoke of our shared history and the potential for a future together.

As we pulled away, Lydie rested her head on my shoulder, and we continued to watch the ripples on the lake's surface in contented silence. The night was peaceful, and in Lydie's company, I felt a sense of belonging and comfort that I hadn't known in years.

Chapter Nine

Lydie

The past three weeks had been a whirlwind of happiness, laughter, and love. Jack and I were officially in a relationship, and every day felt like a beautiful chapter in a love story that was long overdue.

We couldn't resist the temptation of innocent kisses, stolen moments of tenderness that spoke volumes about the affection we held for each other. With each brush of lips, my heart danced, and I couldn't help but feel like a kid again, swept up in the euphoria of first love.

Jack's thoughtfulness and gestures of affection definitely didn't make me feel more mature. Every morning, a sweet "good morning" text from him brightened my day. And on the days we weren't together, a single red rose sent to the bakery awaited me,

For every day that I get to call you my girlfriend, his note would read each time.

"I can't even get the boy I like to remember my name." Isabella pouted.

"Then, he's not worth your time," I told her. "You deserve a good guy."

Like Jack.

Seriously, I was wearing the largest rose-tinted glasses anyone had ever seen.

One night, Date Night had taken an exciting twist as Jack and I found ourselves at the local bowling alley as we prepared for a double date with Sam and Tori. The idea of spending time with my niece and her husband was too great to pass up, and I couldn't help but feel grateful for the way Jack seamlessly fit into our little group.

Sam and Tori had managed to secure a babysitter for their sweet little Adam, and the four of us were ready for a night of fun and friendly competition. As we laced up our bowling shoes and selected our balls, the enthusiasm in the air was contagious.

"So, how's your bowling game, Lydie?" Jack asked with a playful grin.

I chuckled, fully aware that my bowling skills were less than stellar. "Let's just say tonight might really be in God's hands."

Jack's laughter rang out, a warm melody that mingled with the jovial atmosphere around us. His easygoing nature had quickly endeared me so much to him.

As the game commenced, I watched with amusement as Jack lined up his shot, his concentration unwavering. The ball glided down the lane with precision, knocking down the pins with a satisfying crash. He went again for the remainder of the pins and successfully took them down as well. We all clapped at his victory.

"You're up, Lydie." He grinned.

I stepped up to the lane, ball in hand, saying a silent prayer.

At least let me take one down.

Well, it did— from the next lane over. As soon as the ball left my fingers with a flick of my wrist, I knew I made a mistake. With too much force behind my release, and no sense of direction, I released the ball into the air and it skipped from our lane to the next, knocking down two pins.

"That's one way to do it," I heard Jack tease, his words accompanied by a playful wink.

"Does that count?"

"No."

"Darn."

With lightness in the air, we continued the game, and despite my less-than-stellar performance, I was having a blast, and the joy in Jack's eyes mirrored my own.

As the evening wore on, we found ourselves in the final frame. I picked up the ball, determined to end the game on a less embarrassing note than how I started. This time, my aim was true, and the satisfying sound of pins toppling over filled the air.

As I turned to Jack, a gleam of mischief danced in his eyes. "So, who's the bowling champion now?"

"Well, not you." He laughed. "That's the only time tonight you hit the pins in *your* lane."

I shot him a mock glare. "Oh, you're in for it now."

Then I pounced, collapsing on the plastic sofa next to him, and commenced tickling him in the side.

Jack's laughter transformed into a delightful mix of

laughter and protest as my fingers danced across his ribs. "Hey, hey, mercy!"

"Don't get too confident, mister. I might just have to challenge you to a rematch."

Jack's chuckle was a melody that I could listen to for a lifetime.

As the night drew to a close and the bowling alley lights began to dim, I found myself leaning in closer to Jack, and without hesitation, I pressed a gentle kiss to his lips.

And, like the first time we kissed, the world around us seemed to fade away.

Later that same night as I lay alone in bed, my thoughts drifted back to the time when I had fallen in love with Jack for the first time. The memories were a bit hazy, clouded by the passage of time, but I had an inkling that the feelings I had then were not too dissimilar from what I was experiencing now.

As I sat in the quiet of my room, I closed my eyes, letting the past come to life in my mind. And then, like a ray of sunlight breaking through the clouds, I remembered the promise rings. I rose from my bed and walked over to my vanity.

Once I picked up the promise rings, I was transported back to that pivotal moment when Jack had placed the delicate band on my finger. The weight of the metal, the glint of the stone—it had symbolized a commitment that was unwavering, a love that was pure and untainted by the challenges of the world.

Back then, I had known without a doubt how deeply I loved him. The thought of spending the rest of my life with him had filled my heart with hope and joy. The promise we had made to each other, the whispered dreams of a future together—it had all felt so real, so certain.

Burying those rings in the backyard had been a bittersweet moment, a difficult decision that had been guided by the belief that our paths would cross again

As I held the rings in my hand now, I marveled at the passage of time. The innocence of youth had given way to the complexities of adulthood, but the emotions that had bound us together remained as potent as ever.

In this quiet moment, I realized that my feelings for Jack were not confined to the past. The love I had felt as a teenager had evolved and deepened, maturing into something that was even more profound and meaningful. Jack's return to my life had reignited those dormant emotions, reminding me of the bond that had always existed between us.

Jack had grown up, of course, as had I. Life had taken us on separate journeys, filled with challenges, joys, and heartaches.

Yet, in so many ways, he was still *my Jack*—the same boy whose smile could light up a room, whose laughter was infectious, and whose presence made my heart race.

I couldn't deny the growing warmth in my chest, the way my heart seemed to skip a beat every time I thought of him. It was a feeling that I hadn't experienced in years, and I couldn't help but wonder if it was love blossoming all over again.

The thought of a life without Jack in it was inconceivable. He had reentered my world, filling my days with happiness, love, and warmth.

As I lay there, thoughts of the time capsule danced through my mind. I remembered the letters we had written to each other, the ones tucked away in envelopes we promised to open on our wedding day. It was too soon to know for sure, but the thought of what it might be like to open them with him on that day filled me with glee.

Would the words we had penned still hold true today?

In the darkness of my room, I couldn't suppress the smile that tugged at my lips. Love had a funny way of finding its way back into our lives, even when we least expected it.

* * *

It had been a week since our bowling date, but on one random Monday, everything changed.

The ringing of my phone interrupted the usual rhythm of the bakery, and I picked up, expecting to hear Jack's familiar jovial voice.

What I heard instead sent a shiver down my spine.

"Lydie," his voice was weak, and he was sniffling as if he had been crying. Panic gripped my heart, and I immediately abandoned the task at hand, fully focused on the sound of his distress.

"Jack? What's wrong?"

"It's my mom," he choked out, his voice breaking. "She had another stroke. She's in the hospital, Lydie. I... don't think she's doing well."

I felt a rush of emotions—worry, fear, and a sense of helplessness. Viv had only recently reentered his life, and the thought of her being in such a vulnerable state tore at my heart. "Oh, Jack, I'm so sorry. How is she now?"

His reply was a heavy sigh. "She's unresponsive. When we got to the hospital, she wasn't awake. They're doing tests, but... I'm scared."

My heart sank, and I could almost hear the weight of his sadness through the phone.

"I'm on my way," I said without hesitation, my voice resolute. "Jack, I'll be there soon."

Hanging up the phone, I rushed to inform the girls that I needed to leave. Their expressions were filled with understanding and concern, and they encouraged me to go without a second thought. I grabbed my bag, my thoughts a jumble of worry for Viv, and the overwhelming need to be there for Jack.

As I drove to the hospital, the prayers flowed from my lips like a desperate plea.

I prayed for Viv's recovery, for her strength, and for Jack's comfort. The distance between us felt unbearable, and all I wanted was to wrap my arms around him, to offer him whatever solace I could in this difficult moment.

When I arrived, I found Jack standing by a window, his shoulders slumped, and his gaze distant. As I approached him, he turned, and I could see the struggle in his eyes at the effort it took to hold back his tears.

Without a word, I pulled him into a tight embrace, feeling his body shake with suppressed emotion. He held onto me as if I were an anchor in a storm, his grip desperate and vulnerable.

Jack's tears finally broke free, and I held him tighter, offering my support.

"I'm scared, Lydie," he admitted again. "I went to go check on her this morning when I first woke up. She... she got sick on herself, and then... then she just passed out. I... I couldn't..."

"Oh, sweetheart." I gasped, my fingers gently tracing soothing circles on his back. "I'm so sorry. That must have been hard to see. I'm here. And we'll face this... together."

As we sat together in the waiting room, the air heavy with the weight of uncertainty, my thoughts drifted back to a promise I had made to Jack. It was a promise born out of love, and I was willing to do whatever it took to support the person who held my heart.

My love for Jack was a driving force, an unwavering commitment to stand by his side through life's hardest battles.

Amid the uncertainty that loomed over us, Jack turned to me and asked if I would go to the hospital chapel with him.

Without hesitation, I replied, "Absolutely, Jack."

We rose from our seats, our hands instinctively finding each other's in a reassuring grip.

Together, we navigated the labyrinthine hallways of the hospital until we found the chapel, a sanctuary of peace amidst the chaos. The scent of incense filled the air as we stepped inside, the flickering candles casting dancing shadows on the walls.

Jack led the way to a pew, our hands still entwined. The silence of the chapel enveloped us, offering a moment of respite from the turmoil outside. Jack closed his eyes, his lips moving silently in prayer.

I watched him with a heart full of love and admiration. In that sacred space, I could see the vulnerability in his eyes, the weight of his worries, and the depth of his faith. And I knew that being there with him, holding his hand in silent solidarity was exactly what he needed from me

I closed my eyes with Jack as soon as he started to speak his prayer aloud.

"Please, Lord," he started. "I know you have a plan for all of us, but I'm not ready to say goodbye just yet. I promise, one day, I'll let your Holy hands take her, but just not now. Please. There is so much more of my life that I want to share with her."

When I felt him squeeze my hand, I opened my eyes and saw him staring into mine, a genuine smile on his face.

"I want her to see me standing at the altar while my future wife walks to me," he said, his gaze never leaving mine. "I want her to know that I have met, fallen in love, and pledged before you, God, that I will respect and dedicate the rest of my life to her."

We sat side by side in the quiet of the chapel, Jack's prayer-filled words hanging in the air. His vulnerability and the weight of his worries were palpable, but so was his love.

As I watched him, my heart swelled with a love of my own— so profound that it left me almost breathless. At that moment, all I wanted was for Jack to understand how cherished he was, how deeply I cared for him, and how willing I was to do anything for him. But the words eluded me, and I just sat frozen with feeling.

Instead of speaking, I leaned forward and pressed my lips to his. It was a kiss that held all the unspoken emotions, all the love and tenderness I had for him. Our souls connected, and the intensity of our emotions flowed between us.

Our lips finally parted, and we gazed into each other's eyes, the weight of our unspoken confessions hanging in the air.

There was no need for words now, the kiss said it all.

In that sacred chapel, amidst the flickering candles and the cross hanging over us, we rekindled a love once lost to time and distance.

Afterwards, we walked back to the waiting room and sat together in the plastic chairs outside Viv's hospital room.

Every time a doctor or nurse passed by, Jack's grip on

my hand would tighten, his eyes filled with anxiety, and his worry etched deep in the lines of his face. I could feel the tension radiating from him, his fear that they would bring him the dreaded news he didn't want to hear.

I wasn't a doctor, but I knew what it meant to have a stroke that left you unconscious. It wasn't good; if she wakes up, it could mean brain damage and even more restrictive mobility issues for her. It made me agonize in fear for her, and for Jack if the news he received today wasn't good.

The longer we waited, I couldn't help but drift into a stream of memories—fond recollections of Viv, who had been a fixture in my life for as long as I could remember.

Even before Jack and I had started dating, he had been a constant presence in my life. We had spent our formative years playing together, exploring the world with the carefree abandon of childhood. And through it all, Viv and my mother, Rena, had watched over us from their porches, their smiles evidence to the bond that grew between our families.

Vivian had been more than just Jack's mother; she had been a second mother to me as well. Her warm embrace, her comforting presence, and her endless kindness had made her a maternal figure in my life, a source of strength and wisdom that I had leaned on throughout the years, especially after my own mother's passing.

Now, as we faced this uncertain moment, my heart ached with the same sense of helplessness that Jack felt. I wasn't ready to say goodbye to Vivian either. She was more than a friend; she was family. And just like Jack, I clung to the hope that she would recover, that we would continue to share moments of laughter and love, and that she would continue to be a guiding light in our lives.

So, we waited. Praying that the woman we both loved would come back to us.

Chapter Ten

Jack

The more I had to wait for my mother's diagnosis, the more I was convinced the news was going to be bad.

I'd never been particularly fond of hospitals. It always felt cold despite the efforts to make it seem welcoming. White walls, sterile decor, and the faint smell of disinfectant pervaded the air. The sight of needles, the incessant beeping of machines, and the clinical atmosphere were things I could never get used to.

I especially hate it now.

I sat on the edge of the uncomfortable chair, trying to keep my thoughts from wandering into dark places. Yet, as hard as I tried, I couldn't stop the gloomy threads from unraveling.

Walking into mom's room, and seeing her like that. Seeing the vomit – if her head wasn't tilted, she could have choked on it. The way her face was drooped, one lid of her eye sagging, and the corner over her mouth in a deep frown. I had called for her, over and over, in those first few moments. No response. I panicked, but as soon as I realized she was breathing, but unconscious, I called the ambulance.

I had seen things far worse in the military, but this wasn't war, this was my mother.

The doctor that afternoon was taking longer than expected, and the waiting was taking its toll on me.

Before I knew it, my knee was bouncing up and down with anxiety.

Lydie was sitting beside me, her hand firmly holding mine.

"It's going to be okay, Jack," she whispered to me, reassuringly, not for the first time that day.

I looked around the room, trying to distract myself from the fear that gnawed at me. My mind drifted back to the chapel at the church, where I had confessed my love for Lydie in so many words. With her answering kiss, I was sure she felt the same way.

I glanced at her. Her piercing blue eyes met mine, and I couldn't help but smile. She understood the gravity of the situation, but she was here with me, offering her strength.

The door finally opened, and the doctor walked into the waiting area, a serious expression on her face. I felt a lump in my throat as I braced myself for bad news.

"Your mother is stable," she told me. I wanted to feel relieved, but the deep frown on the doctor's face kept me standing still. "She had a hemorrhagic stroke – bleeding in the brain. Thankfully, the bleeding was in the space around her brain, and you got her here soon enough that we were able to find it quickly. I think with the right medications, we can treat this without surgery, but we will need to keep a much closer eye on her from now on.

"She is a strong one, your mother, and she won't let this be the end of her. We're going to need to keep her for a few days for observation. She's asleep right now, but when she wakes up she might have further complications that we will need to address."

My aching heart felt like it was breaking even more, but at least my mom was stable and resting. "Thank you so much, Dr. Avery."

Dr. Avery began explaining the treatment options, the prognosis, and what the future might hold. I listened attentively, absorbing the information, but my thoughts kept drifting back to my mother. I couldn't bear the thought of losing her. I couldn't imagine a world without her.

"She's resting right now," Dr. Avery repeated, "but you can go in and see her."

"Thank you, doctor."

Mom's room was bathed in the antiseptic, fluorescent light that made everything appear stark and lifeless. I stood there, feeling a pang of sadness in my chest as I gazed at the woman sleeping in the bed.

My mother looked so small and fragile, so different from the vibrant woman I had known for most of my life.

The doctor had assured us that she was fine for right now, but that didn't stop the worry from creeping in.

I walked closer to the bed and took her hand in mine. Her skin felt cold against my touch. The veins on the back of her hand stood out, a roadmap of the years she had lived. Wrinkles had gathered at the corners of her eyes, and her face looked sunken, the vibrant colors of her youth now muted.

I traced a finger over the veins on her hand, feeling a

mix of emotions welling up inside me. It was a reminder that even parents, those invincible figures from our childhood, were not immune to the passage of time.

"Mom," I whispered, my voice breaking slightly. "You'll be okay, right?"

Silence.

As I sat by her bedside, Lydie on the other, we fell into a comfortable silence.

I thought about all the sacrifices my mother had made for me, the love and support she had given me throughout my life. She had been there for my first day of school, cheered me on at my high school graduation, and had been my anchor during my years in the military. She was the person I turned to in times of joy and sorrow, and I couldn't imagine my life without her.

Tears welled up in my eyes as I realized that one day, inevitably, I would have to face a world without her. The thought was almost unbearable, and I clung to her hand as if it were the only lifeline keeping me from drowning in a sea of despair.

"Jack," Lydie said softly. "Whatever you need, I'm here for you."

I nodded, unable to find my voice.

"Thank you," I finally croaked.

As I sat there, the rhythmic sound of my mother's breathing filling the space, my mind drifted back to the moment when I had first received news of my mother's failing health. The words on the other end of the line had been laden with sorrow and concern, as the doctor delivered the prognosis: advanced heart failure.

My own heart had clenched in my chest as I listened, struggling to process the gravity of the situation.

I had just come back stateside after being stationed

miles away, deep into my military career. The commitment I had made to serve my country was a calling I had always felt deep within my soul. I was proud to wear the uniform, to stand alongside my comrades, and to do my part to protect the citizens of America. It was a responsibility I took seriously, and I knew that God had put me on this Earth to serve.

But that didn't mean the news hadn't struck me with a heavy dose of frustration and sorrow; after so many years away, I was unaware of how much her health had declined after my father's passing, and coming back now and hearing it all for the first time?

And now, as I watched my mother sleep, her frail form tucked beneath the sterile hospital sheets, I couldn't help but think of all the years I had spent away from her. Her vibrant years had slowly faded into a twilight that I hadn't been there to witness.

I leaned forward, placing a gentle kiss on my mother's forehead as she slept. Her breathing remained steady, and I was happy to hear the sound of it.

In the days that followed, I stayed by my mother's side.

For two days, she remained unconscious, and each day I did not leave the hospital until the nurses dragged me out and told me to come back tomorrow.

"We will alert you as soon as she wakes up, Mr. Weston," they would say to me each night, and each night I drove back to my empty house and wept into my pillow.

I was barely holding on. For those two days, I struggled to sleep, shower, or even put food in my mouth. Lydie, for how wonderful she was, stopped by each morning before she had to be at the bakery, and she would make breakfast.

Practically forcing it down my throat if I told her I wasn't hungry.

"How do you think Viv's going to feel when she wakes up and hears you haven't been eating?" She would guilt me.

And, I fell for it each time. "She'll scold me."

"Exactly. Eat your bacon."

Then, by the grace of God, Mom woke up on that third day. I was sitting by her bedside when her throat croaked and her eyes fluttered open. I called for the nurse immediately.

"Hello, Mrs. Weston," the nurse greeted her. "Would you like to drink some water?"

My mother nodded, and the nurse held a straw to her lips. Once she was done, the nurse checked her vitals and then asked if she knew where she was.

We watched as my mother's eyes danced around the room. She looked confused, and it took her a couple of tries to get the word out.

"Hospital?"

"Very good!" The nurse praised her. "Can you try to wiggle your fingers for me, please?"

Again, it took a second, her eyes knitting together in confusion as she tried to work the muscles on her hand, but then she did, one finger tapping against the mattress.

"Very good, Mrs. Weston! This is good news! Let me go get the doctor." Then, she was gone, and we were alone.

"Jack?" She had asked, looking at me with surprise.

"Yeah, Mom?"

"When did you get back from Iraq?"

"There doesn't seem to be anything wrong with her brain activity," Dr. Avery informed me after she took a couple of

MRIs, looking to see if there was anything wrong with mom's brain activity that could result in the loss of her memory. "I just think her brain is a little scattered right now after the shock. Let's give her a couple of days. If her memory doesn't start to improve, I'll run some more tests."

Shockingly, it didn't take two days for her memory to recover. By late afternoon on the third day, she could recall almost everything except for the few moments before her stroke.

"I just remember not feeling well, and then, I woke up here," she told us.

As the days in the hospital progressed, her favorite TV shows became a form of communication between her and me. Honestly, I didn't watch much television. I liked movies, and I found it hard to keep invested in the complicated storylines of a series. Yet, the more we watched her soap operas, the more I found myself just as enthralled as her.

"Wait." I held up my hand, utterly confused. "I thought Tabitha was married to Sean?"

"No." My mom sighed. "Tabitha is the *ex-wife* of Sean. She's in love with Sean's brother, Dustin, now. She wants to marry him."

"But I thought Dustin was in a coma?"

The look she gave me told me how annoyed she was. "Yes, he is, but they fell in love before the car crash, and before Dustin ended up in a coma."

"Oh," I said like I understood. I didn't.

Besides the dramas, the sporadic visits of Lydie throughout the next few days definitely boosted both mine and my mother's morale. Her visits were a ray of sunshine that we were both lacking inside the confines of the hospital.

"Hello, guys," she would greet every time, a warm smile on her face. "Here, Jack, I brought you some food."

Whether it was a cheeseburger or fries, chicken pot pie, or even a steak cooked medium well, I ate well because of her.

"Ah," my mom pouted, "I want a cheeseburger."

I glared at her. "You just had a stroke. You're not getting a cheeseburger."

"Jack Lawrence, I am your mother. You cannot tell me what I can and cannot have!"

Not giving in, I crossed my arms over my chest. "Fine. Let me go ask Dr. Avery. I bet she'll be on my side. Will you listen to her?"

My mom's pout deepened. "You're mean. A mean, mean son."

I chuckled. "I just want to keep you alive for a very long time."

"Oh trust me," she said. "God and I have talked about it. I'm not going anywhere just yet."

Of course, we couldn't know that for sure, but I had always put my whole faith in God. I had to believe that it was His power that made my mother's recovery so easy.

It felt like a miracle.

When I needed to step away for a brief respite, Lydie willingly sat with my mom while I spent a couple of hours getting myself together.

The nights away from the hospital were lonely and restless. The beeping machines and the faint hum of the hospital's ventilation system were replaced by an eerie silence. The house felt empty without my mother's presence.

While she was with us, Lydie mentioned that the entire town cared for my mother, and I had seen evidence of this during my stay. Neighbors had offered their assistance, friends had sent heartfelt messages of support, and the hospital staff had gone above and beyond to ensure her comfort. She was loved by all.

The day had finally come when my mom was released from the hospital. One week felt like an eternity.

"Just remember," Dr. Avery instructed us firmly before she allowed us to leave the room. "Follow that new diet I charted out for you. No more high cholesterol foods or artificial sugars. Plus, you have some more medications now, so don't forget to take those. And call me if anything changes or if you aren't feeling well. You promise, Mr. and Mrs. Weston?"

"I promise," my mother said, and I seconded that.

Lydie was there to help carry my mom's belongings while I rolled my mother out of the building in her wheelchair.

"I'll see you back at the house," Lydie said, waving goodbye to my mom, and giving me a quick peck on the cheek before heading back to her own car.

As we arrived back at the house, I was taken aback by the sight that greeted us.

The front yard was adorned with colorful decorations, and the air was filled with the sweet scent of freshly baked treats.

"Wow!" My mom gasped, truly delighted. "What is all of this?"

I truly did not have an answer for her.

My mom's eyes sparkled with surprise and gratitude as I helped her out of the truck. At our arrival, neighbors started to trickle out of our front door to greet Mom and to help me wheel her up the steps.

"I'm so glad you're back home, Viv," they said as we passed.

"We love you, Miss Vivian!" Kids squealed from the front yard, playing with water guns and bubble blowers.

Inside, the house was even more astonishing. The transformation was nothing short of remarkable. Balloons of all shapes and colors embellished every corner, their cheerful presence casting a celebratory atmosphere throughout the room. Streamers dangled from the ceiling like colorful ribbons.

Banners hung proudly from every available surface, each one bearing a warm and welcoming message. "Welcome Home, Vivian".

As my mom was wheeled further into the house, her initial exhaustion seemed to dissipate in an instant, replaced with renewed energy and excitement. The sheer magnitude of the decorations overwhelmed her, and she couldn't help but smile.

The room was filled with the sound of laughter and chatter as neighbors and friends mingled. Everyone had come to celebrate my mom's return.

"Jack, did you do all of this?" Mom asked me.

I shook my head. "It wasn't me, but I have a feeling I know who did."

As if my words summoned her, Lydie appeared out of the crowd and approached my side. I reached for her, wrapping my arm around her waist and placing a sweet kiss on her cheek.

"Thank you," I whispered to her.

"Of course," she said back. "I just wanted you and Viv to know that you are loved. We all care about you."

Warmth pricked my eyes, but I didn't want to cry. I had cried so much lately that I didn't even think I could produce the solution anyway.

As I helped my mom settle into a comfortable spot, Tori,

with her young son Adam, stepped up to see mom. My mom's face lit up as she interacted with the energetic child.

"Now, aren't you just the cutest little thing!" Mom squealed, tickling the toddler's belly. Adam laughed loudly, his face red with glee.

As the celebration drew to a close, my mom's eyes shone with gratitude and contentment. She had been surrounded by love and support, and it had filled her heart with joy. Our neighbors had come together to welcome her home, and the sense of belonging was deeply moving.

By the end of the night, I helped my mom settle back into her room. I gave her the new pills Dr. Avery prescribed and helped tuck the covers in around her.

As I kissed my mom goodnight and made my way to the living room, I couldn't help but feel a profound sense of gratitude for everyone that was able to come today.

We were not alone.

As I entered the living room, Lydie was in the process of clearing away all the trash. Empty plates and cups were strewn about, and she moved with a sense of purpose.

Feeling a surge of affection and gratitude, I approached her quietly, not wanting to startle her. With a trash bag in hand, she was focused on her task, her attention on tidying up the space. As I got closer, I gently wrapped my arms around her waist. She responded with a soft gasp. However, her initial surprise quickly turned into relaxation as she leaned back into my hold.

Nuzzling my face into the curve between her shoulder and neck, I inhaled deeply, savoring the comforting scent that always seemed to linger around her. It was a mixture of vanilla and sugar, a fragrance that never failed to soothe my senses.

As we swayed together, the soft strains of music playing

in the background seemed to match the rhythm of our hearts. It wasn't quite dancing, but more like a gentle synchronization of movements. Lydie's hands found their way to my arms, holding onto me.

In that intimate moment, I felt an overwhelming rush of emotions. Gratitude for all that Lydie had done for me and my mother. Affection for the genuine care she had shown, not just during the celebration but in every moment we had spent together.

My heart swelled with these feelings, and as the music continued to play softly, I knew I was ready. Pulling her a little closer, I allowed the words to spill out, my voice soft and sincere. "Lydie, I love you."

Her reaction was giving a radiant smile that illuminated the room. She turned her head slightly, her eyes meeting mine with an intensity that sent shivers down my spine.

Lydie's arms tightened around me, drawing me even closer as if she wanted to make sure that this moment was real, that our feelings were truly mutual. And in that embrace, I could feel her heart beating in tandem with mine in a rhythmic affirmation.

As the song came to an end, we remained locked in each other's arms, our foreheads pressed together, our breaths mingling. And in that tender silence, Lydie said to me, "I love you, too, Jack."

With a gentle kiss to her forehead, I held her just a little tighter, cherishing the moment and the woman who had captured my heart in ways I hadn't thought possible.

As a teenager, I was so sure that we were meant to be together, that our love story was written in the stars. But God had other plans for us.

Yet, one thing remained unchanged—the depth of my love for Lydie. It had never wavered, never dimmed, even after all these years. I had never stopped thinking about her, never stopped carrying her memory in my heart.

Over the decades, I had made excuses for why we couldn't be together. Military service, duty, responsibilities—all of them had kept me from pursuing the love I had always known was there. But that night, as I held her close, I realized that I couldn't keep making excuses.

Our love story had taken a long and winding road, filled with heartache and missed opportunities, but it was far from over.

The future was uncertain, but I was certain of one thing—I wanted to experience it all with Lydie by my side.

No more excuses, no more missed opportunities. She was the one I wanted to share my life with, to face whatever came our way.

As we swayed gently to the music, I realized that the love we had was rare and precious. It had endured distance, time, and even my own stubbornness. Now that I had her back in my life, I wasn't about to let go. I was committed to making every moment count, to cherishing the love we had.

I could do anything, as long as she was with me.

Chapter Eleven

Lydie

For the first few weeks after her stroke, Viv needed a lot of care. At first, she was mostly bedridden, only able to do a short walk to and from the bathroom. Jack hired her an additional nurse, someone she would be comfortable assisting with her personal needs, but other than that, Jack was with her 24/7. And, I was right there with him.

As soon as I said those three words, I knew that I wanted to take care of him and his family; plus, being able to spend time with Viv was a real treat in itself.

I'd always show up after closing up the store with some dessert I made that was approved on her diet list, shoo Jack away to go take a shower or nap, and then she and I would just sit for hours, talking about anything and everything.

"Did you know I used to be a dancer?" she asked me one night. My eyes widened in surprise.

"Really? A dancer?"

"Oh, yes, I used to be a part of a little group in Texas. I was maybe twenty, I think? It was before I met Jack's father. There were thirteen of us, six girls, six guys, and one chaperone. We'd travel from town to town and dance in halls or at events for money. It was quite fun."

I was so invested in the story, I had leaned in closer from my chair, my elbows propped up on the side of her bed.

"Did you know a lot of the dances?" My eyebrows knitted as I tried to remember the name. "Oh, like the jitterbug?"

"Yes, like the jitterbug, but my favorite is the swing. If you have a good partner, all of the spinning kind of feels like you're flying."

The side of my lips quirked up, slyly. "A good partner, huh? Viv, did you have a boyfriend before Mr. Weston?"

Her cheeks reddened and she let out a little puff of breath from between her lips. "Not all of us can wait over thirty years for a little romance, Lydie."

I gasped. "Did you... did you just make a joke at my expense?"

"Of course not, dear, I would never."

"Wow, I never thought the great Viv Weston could be such a mean girl."

I couldn't help it, I had to know more. I got just a little bit closer and whispered only for her to hear. "So, what was his name? What happened?"

Viv shrugged, but her expression started to get lofty as she was taken back to a period of time only she could see. "Well, I met Steve, and he just overturned my world. Ted was great, but I didn't get butterflies with him like I did when I was in the same room as Steve. So, Ted and I broke up, and I started dating Jack's father.

"Love has a way of surprising you, Lydie," she continued, looking at me. "Sometimes, it's draining, and it can be hard, but if you have a good partner, you can weather any storm together. In all of the years of our marriage, I can't tell you how many times I got frustrated with Steve, but at the end of the day, I still wanted his forehead kisses. No matter how mad I got, I never got angry enough to leave. I knew that even in times of difficulty, I wanted to be by his side."

She reached out for my hand, and I gave it to her. She patted it gently before holding it tight.

"I am so grateful to you, Lydie. Jack deserves a good, godly woman like you. Thank you for being here. Jack doesn't want to admit it, but he's exhausted. Having you here puts him at ease."

My eyes burned with the nicety of her words. I placed my other hand on top of hers. It worried me how paper thin her skin was.

"I love your son very much, Viv," I told her, empathetically. "I always have."

Viv started showing wonderful progress with the physical therapy she was receiving twice a week

First, Stacy, her therapist, helped her with her upper body strength, getting her fingers to wiggle for longer than a few seconds, then her grip, and as soon as she was sitting up on her own without pillows propping her up, Stacy started helping her stand.

Jack was almost insufferable during this time.

He and Stacy worked together to keep Viv steady and moving, but every time she stumbled or fell into Jack's arms, he would tense up.

"Maybe that's enough today," he would always suggest.

Viv would give him an exasperated look. "Stacy hasn't even been here for thirty minutes, honey. I want to keep going."

Jack would argue. "She's coming back on Thursday. You can do more then."

Then, lastly, Viv would win. She'd put her hands on her hips and give Jack a stern look that only works on sons. "Jack Weston, I am going to do this physical therapy. You can either stay and help, or leave. Lydie can take your place."

Scolded as he always was, Jack would apologize.

"It's okay. Now, if you so please, I'd like to make it to the other side of the room before nightfall, so, scoot! Let's go."

It wasn't until Viv was able to make it around her room without any assistance that Jack started to withdraw.

Jack's new mood left me perplexed and uneasy. He constantly seemed distracted, his thoughts drifting into a realm that he wasn't willing to share. Every time I asked if he was okay, he would offer a half-hearted reassurance, but I could sense the truth in his eyes – something was amiss, and he was keeping it from me.

Doubts gnawed at me, and I couldn't help but wonder if I was the problem. Did he regret confessing his feelings for me? I tried not to let those dark thoughts sink in, but the amount of times it seemed like he was dodging me, I couldn't think of it to be anything else.

As the days progressed and his mood wasn't improving, I decided to confide in my sister, Mira. I called her on a Thursday after I locked up the bakery for the night.

She answered on the first ring.

"Mira," I said in a way of greeting, my heavy heart speaking volumes that I couldn't express.

"Oh, no," she said, her tone reflecting mine. "What happened? Is everything okay? Is it Jack's mother?"

She listened attentively as I poured out my concerns about Jack's recent behavior.

"He just... I don't know, it seems like he doesn't want me around."

"You know, Lydie," Mira said thoughtfully, "sometimes people withdraw when they're going through a tough time. It might not be about you at all. It could be about his mom."

I considered her words carefully. Jack's mother's failing health was definitely not something neither he nor I were willing to take lightly, but there was still that intuition in the pit of my stomach that this was not that.

"Maybe," I said, slowly, "but Viv's been doing so well, and after she finished PT last week, Jack was so happy, and he's been happy up until a few days ago. I just can't help but think it might be something else."

Mira sighed in contemplation. "Well, it could just be stress and burnout. It's not easy to care for someone else, and Jack seems like the type to put others' needs above his own. It'd probably be a good idea to get him out of the house, do something fun with him to take his mind off of things."

"But what can I do to help him?" I asked, my voice tinged with worry.

Mira's response was swift and filled with sisterly affection. "What about the Fall Carnival? Beaufort still does that, right? Why don't you take him there? It could be really fun."

That was such a good idea. When we were younger, Jack and I had spent date nights at the Fall Carnival. There were probably so many memories wrapped up in that festival. I'd love to take him and Viv, get them out of the confines of their home.

A few days later, I surprised Jack with the plan. I could see a flicker of surprise and delight in his eyes as I told him about our day at the carnival. It was the first smile I saw on his lips in the last twenty-four hours.

I was even more happy when he got up from the chair he was sitting in and gave me a big, warm hug. I relished in the physical contact, holding onto him longer than the intimacy called for.

"That's so great, Lydie. I'll let Mom know. She loves the carnival. Plus, her new scooter just came in, so I know she's been wanting to try it."

So, in that second week of September when the summer heat finally started to break and the leaves were falling, we planned our carnival adventure.

We packed Viv up in Jack's SUV, and he wrestled with fitting her scooter in the back. It was a great piece of machinery that was easy to use, even with Viv's mobility issues. She had no issue using the little joystick to get the scooter moving; plus, the seat was extra comfy and padded for support. Thankfully, the fairgrounds were mostly paved over with concrete so she would have no problem getting around.

At the fairgrounds, Jack pulled into a handicap parking spot at the front of the entrance, and there, waiting for us on the sidewalk was Tori and her family. Viv expressed interest in seeing little Adam again, so I called up Tori with plans for our carnival day, and she couldn't be more excited.

"Ohh, Adam loves the carnival!" she squealed through the phone once I told her. "Let me make sure Sam isn't busy, and we'll all go."

"Hey, man," Sam greeted Jack with a hearty handshake as soon as he opened the back of the car. "Need any help?"

Jack beamed with appreciation. "Sure, if you don't mind helping me get my mother's scooter down. It can be a bit heavy."

Together, the men pulled the scooter out of the trunk and got it situated before I helped Lydie out of the backseat. As soon as she was settled on the scooter, she reached out for Adam who was tilting out of his mom's arms in her direction.

"He absolutely loves you!" Tori confessed to Viv. "It's so cute."

She handed her son over, and he sat happily perched on Viv's lap. She wrapped a protective arm around his belly and used her other hand to steer the scooter. We wasted no time after that to buy our tickets and enter the grounds.

Crisp leaves crunched beneath my feet as we strolled through the bustling fairgrounds. The air carried the aroma of warm apple cider, sugary treats, and overly greased french fries.

Twinkling lights lit every corner. The carousel's cheerful melodies echoed in the air, and the Ferris wheel stood tall over everything else. Laughter and joyful screams created a symphony of excitement, punctuated by the occasional ring of bells from game stalls.

As I wandered hand in hand with Jack, the chill in the air was tempered by the warmth of shared smiles. Pumpkin decorations furnished booths, and the atmosphere felt like a canvas painted with the colors of fall.

Later, as the day progressed, we rode the Ferris wheel together, and I couldn't help but steal glances at Jack, his profile illuminated by the carnival lights. There was a moment of serenity in his expression, a respite from the weight of his concerns. I could tell he was happy, even if underneath the surface a war still brewed in his mind. We indulged in carnival treats, sharing cotton candy, and trying our luck at various games. Our laughter filled the air as we took part in the day, surrounded by family and happiness.

As the day drew to a close, we found ourselves in front of a grand carousel, its ornate horses and whimsical music inviting us to step into a world of enchantment. We climbed onto the bright horses, waiting for the ride to start.

"Hey, Jack?"

"Yeah?"

I felt nervous asking, but I did so anyway. "Is everything okay? You seem... a bit down lately."

He gave me a smile that didn't match his eyes. "Yeah, everything is fine. I'm so happy you thought to bring us here. Mom and I really needed it. We owe so much to you, Lydie. I hope you know that."

I smiled, but his words didn't reassure me. They felt more like a vague answer, a brush-off to keep me from asking any more questions.

"You know I'm here for you, right?" I asked him. "I... I love you."

This time when he smiled, it was genuine. "I know, and I love you. So much. I promise I'm fine. Just have a lot on my mind."

Then, he reached across the space between us and took my hand. For the rest of the ride, we enjoyed it in silence, both of us caught up in our thoughts.

The front door clicked softly behind me as I stepped into the quietness of my home.

Jack had returned to his quiet self on the drive back

from the carnival, his eyes distant like he was worlds away. The merry-go-round music and twinkling lights felt like they belonged to another time and place. Together, he and I got Viv's scooter out of the back and helped Viv inside. As usual, he insisted on walking me across the street to my front door.

"I had a great time today, Lydie. Thank you," he said, the smile almost touching his eyes.

"I'm glad, Jack."

He stood there, then, looking at me, and for a moment I thought he was going to finally let me into whatever war was raging inside of his mind, but then he kissed me gently on my cheek and said,

"Goodnight, Lydie."

"Oh," I said, trying to not let the disappointment ring out in my voice. "Good night, Jack."

Then, he was gone.

I kicked off my shoes and hung my purse on the hook, but my thoughts remained tethered to the concerned look in Jack's eyes when he said goodnight.

"Why won't he talk to me?" I muttered to myself, making my way through the dimly lit hallway. "I can't help him if he won't let me in."

Randomly, I thought of Gus and wished I still had his warm, furry body to curl up next to, but his family came back from their vacation two weeks ago, and I was once again left by myself. Life really does feel better with a cat.

Reaching my bedroom, I felt a sudden tightness in my chest. I sat down on the edge of my bed, my gaze falling on the Bible that lay on my bedside table.

My heart knew where to find solace. I picked it up and opened it to the Psalms, always a balm when my soul was uneasy.

"God," I began softly, my hands gently resting on the opened Book. "You know the heaviness in Jack's heart, the burdens he's unwilling to share with me. I pray for your peace to flood his soul. I pray for wisdom in his decisions, for strength in his moments of weakness."

A sense of calm enveloped me, a reassuring warmth that only Faith can bring. I took a deep breath, my eyes moistening. "I want to stand beside him, Lord, through every test and trial. Please show me how to be a pillar of support, even when he pushes me away."

I sighed, feeling the weight of my own words. Loving someone was like the rides at the carnival; it wasn't all laughter and thrill. Sometimes it was silence, long drives home filled with unspoken worries, and quiet prayers in the dead of night.

"Help him find his way back to You, God. And help me to love him the way You love us—fully, unconditionally, and without end. Amen."

Closing my Bible, I felt an unwavering belief that my prayer hadn't fallen on deaf ears. God was at work, even in the stillness, even in the uncertainty. And with that assurance, I crawled under the covers, my heart a bit lighter, knowing that love—both Divine and earthly—would see us through the battles yet to come.

With that final thought, my eyes drifted closed, giving way to dreams that were prayers in their own right—visions of brighter days, open hearts, and a love that could weather any storm.

Chapter Twelve

Jack

I received the call on Thursday.
I stared at my phone as Mason's voice cut through the background noise of my life.

That sinking sensation, that ominous feeling of dread in the pit of my stomach clawed its way back. It had been weeks, beautiful weeks, where I'd felt lighter than air, basking in the happiness that Lydie had brought into my life and that my mother's condition was improving.

Yet, this one phone call, Marcus's name displayed on the screen, made my adrenaline spike with unease. There was only one thing Marcus asks when he calls, and Jack didn't want to have to give him an answer, not this time.

I should have ignored it.
But I didn't.
"Hello?" I answered on the last ring.
"Lieutenant Colonel? Jack, is that you?"

Who else would it be?

"Yeah, hi, Marcus. What's up? I can't stay on the phone long. I have to get my mother her lunch."

"Jack. Jim's dead."

For a moment, I lost the ability to speak, too stunned to say anything at all. That was not at all what I was expecting him to say.

"Jack? Are you listening?"

My mind snapped back to the conversation. "Yeah, Mason, I heard you," I replied, my voice hollow and distant even to my own ears.

Jim Doer was a good man, probably served as long as I did, if not more. He was loyal and strong in the field and an even better friend. The guy who had gotten me through some of the toughest times during deployment, and he was gone.

"What happened?" I managed to ask, my voice cracking with sorrow.

Mason proceeded to recount the details of the accident. Jim had been on his way home from work when a drunk driver had plowed into his car.

"He was dead before the ambulance even got there."

I was still clutching my phone, my knuckles white.

The news of his death was like a punch to the gut. It ripped through the serenity I'd found in Beaufort.

It completely shattered it when Mason voiced the question I had dreaded him asking.

"So, you know Jim always wanted to do one more tour before retiring, right?" he asked. "I talked with the others, and we want to do another enlistment, in honor of Jim. We want you to be there with us, Lieutenant Colonel. It would have meant so much to Jim to be able to serve with you."

That sinking feeling dropped completely to the bottom of my stomach and stayed there like a heavy weight.

If it had been any other time, I wouldn't have hesitated. I loved my career and the responsibility that came with it, and I loved serving with my fellow sisters and brothers, but this time felt different. There were different factors to consider that hadn't been there in the past, and that was what brought me so much anxiety. The fact that I had to choose one over the other.

My career.

Or, my mother and Lydie.

I didn't know how to make that choice; I especially didn't have the answer Marcus wanted to hear.

"Oh, uh, uhm." I struggled to string a sentence together. "Sorry, Marcus, can I call you back? My mother is calling for me."

"What? Oh, yeah, sure, man. Hey, just let me know at the funeral, okay? Registration closes that following Monday."

"Yeah, definitely, I'll call you, bye."

I dropped my phone on the counter like it was a toxin and stepped away from it, controlling my breathing as much as I could and trying to calm myself. My fingers started to go numb, but my hands were shaking. I could see them in front of me, but I had no ability to control them.

Breathe. Breathe. Breathe.

I repeated this to myself multiple times as I tried to slow my racing heart. I felt overwhelmed. My mother's stroke. Jim's death. The fear of letting everyone down if I chose to go overseas again. It was too much.

In the days that followed Mason's call, I couldn't escape the war that waged within my own mind, each side fighting for dominance, and there was no clear victor in sight.

Chapter Twelve 127

I was torn between two worlds, two responsibilities, and two forms of love.

On one hand, it was my duty to my country.

I had spent years serving in the military, defending the values and freedoms that America stood for. It was a commitment I had willingly made, and one I took with pride. The news of Jim's death weighed heavy on my heart, not just because he was a fellow soldier, but because he was a friend. We had endured hardships together, laughed in the face of danger, and shared our dreams of the future. To abandon my platoon in their time of mourning felt like a betrayal of the deepest kind.

On the other side were Lydie and my mother.

The past few months had been a revelation, a resurgence of feelings and desires I had long buried underneath my patch. Lydie's presence had breathed life into my world, a world that had grown gray and cold over the years without her. Her love had become a beacon of warmth. Was I going to risk that? My mother's need for support and care weighed heavily on me as well. She had gotten much better recently; so much so that she had been taken off of hospice care, but she still needed daily assistance. She would not be able to take care of herself, was I really going to abandon her?

As I stood at the crossroads, I didn't know which path to choose. I knew that if I refused the call to march in Jim's honor, I would regret it. My platoon was family, and this is what we do to pay our respects.

Days turned into nights, and I became more withdrawn, lost in the turmoil of my own thoughts. Lydie sensed the change in me, her concerned glances and gentle touches a constant reminder that I couldn't hide forever. But the words remained trapped, unspoken, and heavy.

What if I told her and she was angry? What if she left me

again, but this time for good? It was a fear that gnawed at me, that kept me silent when I should have confided in her.

At the carnival, I tried to be happy, and for the most part, I was. I loved that mom was enjoying herself, the feel of Lydie's hand in mine, and the good energy that came from being around family, but the later the night got, the more worn down I came.

By the time we left the fairgrounds and got my mother back in bed for the night, I was emotionally exhausted. I kissed Lydie good night as I walked her across the street to her home.

That night, I didn't sleep at all.

When my alarm went off the next morning, I had to drag myself out of bed. My eyes burned with lack of sleep, and my mind felt clouded. I went through the motions of preparing my mother's breakfast and her medications. She was already up and waiting for me by the time I opened her door.

"Good morning, sweetie."

"Morning, Mom."

I handed Mom her breakfast tray and her morning pills. She smiled, a warmth in her eyes that never dimmed no matter how frail her body became.

Turning away, I went to the bedroom window. Beyond the curtain, I saw the row of old oak trees and the lake that shimmered behind it. A quiet stillness settled over me as memories flooded back. Running through these woods, fishing by the lake with Dad, that first kiss with Lydie on the shore when we were sixteen.

Beaufort was still home, even if it'd been years since I'd lived here.

A deep exhale escaped my lips. Tired didn't begin to describe how I felt.

"Jack." Mom's voice broke into my thoughts. "When are you going to tell me what's been bothering you these last few weeks?"

I didn't turn around at her question, too much of a coward to look her in the eye.

"Mom, it's nothing you need to worry about."

I heard her snort behind me. "You can't fool me. There's more in your eyes than just exhaustion, honey. Come on, tell me. Maybe I can help."

I sighed, hesitating before the dam broke. "A friend of mine from the platoon, Marcus, called to tell me another friend died. The crew is thinking about doing another tour to honor him."

I finally faced her and she nodded for me to continue.

"I'm torn, Mom. After your last stroke, the idea of leaving you alone..." I choked. I couldn't stand the thought of not being here with her.

Her hand reached for mine, and I walked back to her. "Jack, if you feel that's where the Lord wants you, then you shouldn't hold yourself back on my account. He'll take care of me, just as He takes care of you."

"But, Lydie...I don't know how to tell her...and, I don't even know if I can leave her. I know what I want and what the Lord wants, but I love her so much, Mom. Is it selfish of me to just want to be with her?"

She shook her head. "You and Lydie have such a beautiful love. I can understand why you wouldn't want to leave that. You have a heavy choice, but I want you to know something."

Mom's eyes softened as she continued. "If Lydie loves you—and I know she does—she'll understand that you have a duty, not just to your platoon, but to yourself. Love isn't only about holding on, Jack; it's about having the strength to let go sometimes."

I squeezed Mom's hand, feeling the wisdom in her touch and the love in her eyes. Whatever path I chose, I knew I wouldn't walk it alone.

And for the first time in days, that thought brought me peace.

I pulled a chair up next to her bed, both of us wrapped in a comfortable silence. My thoughts drifted back to Lydie —her laugh, the way her eyes sparkled when she was passionate about something, the strength she showed even when times got tough.

"Mom," I began, my voice tinged with vulnerability, "how did you know Dad was the one?"

She looked thoughtful, her eyes focusing on some distant point, pulling memories from a different lifetime. "We just knew. It wasn't something magical or sudden. It was in the simple things—the way he made coffee just the way I liked it, how he'd hold me when I was sad, the way we faced problems together. I just woke up one day, and I just knew — I knew that no matter what, I would stand by him and support him no matter what."

I took that in, letting each word settle deep within me. Lydie had been my rock, and I wanted to be hers.

Would love sustain us, like it had sustained Mom and Dad if I left again?

"What about if you had to say goodbye to him, even if just for a little bit?" I pressed, needing to hear more.

Mom smiled gently. "Goodbyes are always hard, but the good thing about a goodbye is the hello that follows. That made the time apart bearable, sometimes even more meaningful."

I nodded, feeling a knot of tension unravel. If I chose to reenlist, there would be goodbyes, tough times ahead, but there would also be reunions, moments of joy to savor.

Picking up my phone, I scrolled to Lydie's name. My thumb hovered over the call button, a mixture of fear and anticipation churning within me. With one last look at Mom, who gave me an encouraging nod, I pressed the call button.

Chapter Thirteen

Lydie

As soon as I saw Jack's number light up my screen, I answered it immediately.

"Jack, hi, is everything okay? Is your mom okay?"

He chuckled lightly on the other end. "Yes, she is fine. I was just calling to see if you wanted to come over for a movie tonight. I miss you."

"You saw me yesterday," I tease, but still, I smiled. "But yes, I would love to come over and watch a movie."

"Great! I'll see you tonight, darling."

"See you tonight, handsome."

After we hung up, I felt marginally better. Jack sounded good for the first time in the last week like he was happy. I wondered if whatever was burdening him had finally come to pass, and for the rest of the day I lived in this little bubble of bliss, looking forward to tonight and getting to see that smile I loved so much on Jack's face.

The last customer of the day waved goodbye, and I flipped the "Open" sign to "Closed".

"Okay, girls," I addressed my staff. "Let's get this place shut down and get out of here! Phew, today was a busy one."

"*All* days here are busy, Lydie."

"I don't hear you complaining when we split up the tips at the end of the night, Isabella." Claudia reminded her.

"Yeah, you are right; plus, Lydie makes us treats before we go!"

I smiled. The scent of freshly baked cinnamon rolls still filled the air, a cozy thank you to the staff I couldn't run this place without. As the girls dug into their rolls, we wiped down the counters, turned off the ovens, and locked up for the night.

I bid each one of them good night and rushed to my car. I parked my car in my driveway and made a pit stop at my house first. I was sweaty from working so close to the ovens, I had flour on my pants, and I'm pretty sure there was frosting in my hair.

Upstairs, I chose a cute and comfortable outfit, light jeans, and a fluffy pink sweater. I jumped in the shower real quick, found out that I did have icing in my hair, and cleaned it out. Out of the water, I blow-dried my hair, spritzed myself with my favorite perfume, and put on my favorite pieces of jewelry.

I was out the door and across my street in half an hour's time.

As I approached, I noticed the front porch light was already on. I knocked softly, and almost immediately, Jack swung the door open, his face lighting up at the sight of me.

"Hey, Lydie," he greeted, stepping aside to let me in and giving me a sweet kiss on the cheek. "You look like you had a good day."

"I did," I said, catching a whiff of buttered popcorn in the air as I entered. "But now, it's about to get even better."

I walked back to the living room, greeted Viv who was joining us from her comfy cocoon of blankets, and plopped down on one of the other couches. Jack sat with me on the same couch.

"How are you doing, Viv?" I asked. Jack put his arm on my shoulders, and I scooted in close to him.

"I'm doing well, dear, better if my son would let me have some popcorn."

I watched as Jack's eyes zeroed in on his mother. "I offered to pop you some!"

"No," she glared back, "you offered to pop me that nasty bland kind. I want the regular kind!"

"You can't have the regular kind. It's loaded with butter and salt! Now, behave."

"Jack Lawrence, I am your mother. You don't tell *me* to behave! I tell you to behave! So... behave!"

"Do you want to watch the movie or not? Because if you keep arguing with me like this, we never will."

Viv huffed, but she didn't say anything else.

Jack and I settled onto his plush, well-worn couch, bowls of popcorn, and our favorite fizzy drinks on the coffee table in front of us. He threw a warm blanket over the both of us, and I rested my head into his shoulder. Jack took the remote and hit play.

As we watched the movie, I noticed Jack seemed more relaxed than he had been lately, laughing at the comical parts and silently engrossed during the poignant moments.

The movie was great, but what was even more funny

was the slight snores coming from Viv. As soon as we looked over at her, she was fast asleep.

Jack laughed. "You know, she argued with me that she wanted to see this movie. I told her it was about two hours long, and she wouldn't make it the whole way through. She insisted that she could."

"How is it with her?" I asked, my voice laced with concern.

The bakery had been so busy lately with the turn of the season. Fall has always been the craziest. I made a lot of seasonal treats and used my own coffee brew that everyone loved. Because of this, I didn't get many days away from the bakery, and by the end of the night, I was so exhausted that I just wanted to crawl into my bed and sleep. I didn't have much energy to spare, so I'd been away from the Weston house for a bit. As a result, I was not up to date on his mother's recovery.

He looked up, his eyes meeting mine. "She's doing great, actually. She has an appointment with Dr. Avery tomorrow, but I'm pretty sure it's going to be good news."

Relief washed over me like a wave. "That's wonderful to hear."

"Yeah," Jack said, before looking at his mother's sleeping form. "I'm going to help get her to bed, but when I come back, there's something I'd like to talk to you about, if that's okay?"

My heart skipped a beat.

Could this be the moment when Jack finally opens up about what's been bothering him lately? "Of course," I said, trying to sound casual.

He disappeared down the hallway, with his mother in his arms, leaving me alone with my thoughts. Minutes felt like hours until I heard his footsteps approaching. Jack returned, his face carrying a blend of seriousness and vulnerability I hadn't seen in a while.

"I'm back," he said, sitting next to me. "Thanks for waiting."

"Always," I replied, reaching for his hand. "So, what's on your mind?"

Jack sighed, running his fingers through his hair. "I found out that an old military buddy of mine passed away."

"Oh, Jack, I'm so sorry," I said, my heart aching for him.

He nodded, swallowing hard. "Yeah, it's been rough, but that's not everything."

As Jack sat next to me on the couch, a somber expression clouding his usually radiant face, I braced myself for what was about to unfold. "We served together, went through the thick and thin of it all."

"I'm so sorry, Jack," I repeated.

He nodded, gathering himself. "Jim always talked about doing one more tour. Said he had more to give, you know? Now my old platoon wants to do a tour in his honor. They want me to join them."

The words hit me like a gust of wind, unexpected and disorienting.

"I don't feel right saying no to them, Lydie," Jack continued, his voice laced with vulnerability. "But I also know that my decisions affect you now. And God knows I've been down that road before, leaving people behind for duty's call. I can't—won't—do to you again what I did all those years ago. I, especially, don't want to wait another thirty years to see you."

My heart ached at the gravity of his confession. He was a man caught between the man he once was and the man he wanted to be—for himself, for me, and for us.

He looked at me then, his eyes earnest and a little fearful. "If you tell me not to go, Lydie, I won't. I'll stay. That's how much you mean to me."

Stunned by the weight of his words, I took a deep breath.

It would be so easy to say, "Stay," to keep the man I loved safe and close. But deep down, I knew what I had to do and what God would want me to do.

"Jack," I said softly, squeezing his hand for emphasis. "I can't make that decision for you, but I can stand by you while you make it. I don't want you to let your platoon down. More importantly, I don't want you to let yourself down. If honoring Jim in this way is what you feel called to do, then who am I to stand in the way of that calling?"

His eyes searched mine as if looking for a sign of hesitation or regret. But all he would find was love and support.

"Are you sure?" he asked.

"As sure as I've ever been about anything," I replied, my heart swelling with a peace only faith could bring. "Love means giving each other the freedom to follow God's path, even when it seems impossible. And I love you, Jack. I would do anything for you, even if that means waiting for you to come back to me."

Jack pulled me into his arms, holding me tightly. "I love you, too, Lydie, more than words could ever express. And I thank God every day for bringing you into my life."

As I held onto Jack, feeling the steady beat of his heart against mine, I sent up a prayer of surrender and trust. *Lord, guide us through this journey, no matter how challenging or painful it might be. Help us to honor You in all that we do, trusting that Your plans are greater than ours.*

And as we sat there, wrapped in the comfort of our love and faith, I knew that whatever came next, we would face it together with courage and honesty.

After a while, Jack sighed. "I've been so worried you'd be upset, maybe even consider ending things."

"That's not how love works," I said softly.

Jack grasped my hand, squeezing it gently as if holding onto a lifeline. "I love you, Lydie."

"And I love you," I replied, my heart swelling with a blend of compassion and understanding. "Whatever comes next, we'll face it together."

He leaned in, his lips meeting mine in a tender kiss.

Later that night, Jack asked me to go with him to Jim's funeral, and I knew there was only one answer. "Of course, I'll be there."

Jack took care of everything, even arranging for his mother's care while we were away.

"Go, go, go," Viv basically shooed him out the door that Thursday morning. "Please, Kate and I are going to have a lovely time."

Kate was the elderly woman down the street who owned five chihuahuas and loved singing loud and off-key while she watered her garden. Seriously, lovely woman, but it was like cats fighting when she sang. When Jack told his mother he wanted to attend Jim's funeral, she told him to call up the woman.

"She's been dying to get at my blueberry lemonade recipe," Viv told us. "She'll come."

So, once Viv was successful at getting Jack out the door, we hit the road, Florida bound. By the time the sun dipped behind the trees on the highway, we finally pulled into the hotel parking lot.

Jack had booked separate rooms for us, handing me my keycard with a proud smile on his face.

"I asked the front desk if we could get rooms next to the

vending machines," he informed me. "I know you love to snack."

I giggled as we made our way down the hallway. "You know me so well."

It was late, so with a quick kiss, Jack went to his room, and I went to mine.

The following morning came all too soon. I dressed in a modest black dress, pausing in front of the mirror to take a steadying breath.

"Lord, give Jack strength today," I whispered.

Soon after, we made our way to the church.

It was a small, whitewashed building, with a humble wooden cross perched above the entrance. A few tall trees framed the church, their leaves rustling in a gentle welcome.

The moment we stepped inside, I couldn't help but feel that we were in God's good hands.

The pews were simple, crafted from aged oak that had witnessed countless prayers and hymns. Stained glass windows, allowing rays of sunlight to filter through, casting a soft, colorful glow on the worn carpet.

The altar was unpretentious, a simple wooden table draped in white cloth with a Bible carefully placed in the center. Above it hung another cross, this one made of darker wood, its grain intricate and beautiful, yet without any ostentation.

"Welcome," an older man greeted us, his eyes crinkling at the corners as he smiled. He had the look of someone who had been a part of this congregation for decades, and his serene countenance only reinforced the feeling of peace I'd felt since we arrived.

"Thank you for having us, pastor," Jack said, holding his hand out for a shake. The man took it gracefully.

As we sat down in the pews, I took a moment to breathe in the atmosphere. I looked over at Jack, his face set in an expression of contemplative solemnity, and I realized how important it was for him to be here, surrounded by a community that shared his grief.

As the organist began to play the opening hymn, I felt Jack take my hand, his fingers weaving through mine in a grateful clasp. After the song, the pastor stepped up to the altar.

He said, "Ladies and gentlemen, family and friends, we gather here today not just to mourn the loss of Jim Doer, but also to celebrate a life well-lived. A life devoted to service and honor.

"You see, Jim was not just a member of our congregation, but he was also a committed military man. He wore his uniform not just as a job but as an emblem of the principles he held dear: courage, integrity, and a love for his country that was second only to his love for God.

"He was a man who didn't just talk about doing the right thing; he lived it. Whether he was serving overseas in conditions most of us could hardly imagine, or back here at home offering a helping hand to his neighbors, Jim was someone you could count on. And today, as we grapple with the painful void his departure has left in our hearts, we are also filled with a sense of gratitude for having known a man of such remarkable caliber."

"Here, here," some whispered.

Sniffles and nods from those who didn't have the words to speak.

"But we are not here to dwell in sorrow," the pastor continued. "Jim would not have wanted that. We are here to find comfort in the arms of our Lord, our Savior, who assures us that in His Father's house are many rooms; He has gone ahead to prepare a place for us. We take solace in knowing that Jim has already embarked on that journey to eternal peace, led there by his unwavering faith.

"And what about us? What can we take away from Jim's life that can serve as a beacon in our own? I would say, my dear brothers and sisters, let us take away the idea that a life of service is a life that brings us closer to God's eternal glory.

"In Matthew 25:40, the Lord says, "Truly I tell you, whatever you did for one of the least of these brothers and sisters of mine, you did for me."

The pastor then held up his hand, closed his eyes, and bowed his head. We all followed suit.

"Let us pray. Heavenly Father, we thank You for the time we had with Jim, for the lessons he taught us, and the love he shared with us. Lord, we ask that You embrace him in Your loving arms, grant him the peace that surpasses all understanding, and comfort those of us who mourn his loss. In Jesus' name, we pray. Amen."

"Amen," rang the congregation.

"Jim Doer may have left this Earth, but his spirit, his legacy, and the indelible marks he left on each of us remain. And so, as we say our final goodbyes today, let us remember him as a man who lived by faith, who served with honor, and who loved without bounds. In this way, he shall remain eternally alive in our hearts.

"May God bless you all, and may God forever hold Jim in the palm of His hand. Amen."

"Amen," we said again.

After the service, I could feel the heaviness in Jack's steps, but when we walked across the graveled drive to the reception hall, something shifted.

His old platoon was there, a band of brothers and sisters who had fought, laughed, and cried together. And for the first time in weeks, I saw the cloud lift ever so slightly from Jack's eyes.

He introduced me to them one by one. These were the people he had served with, the comrades who knew a version of Jack I was only beginning to understand.

"And this is Lydie," Jack would say, pulling me a little closer each time. "She's my girlfriend."

Lastly, he introduced me to Marcus. Jack clapped a hand on his shoulder and said, "I've kept you waiting for an answer, and I'm sorry for that. But yes, I'll reenlist for the new year. An honor march for Jim. One last tour before I retire."

"That's so good to hear, Lieutenant! I'll let the others know."

Marcus grinned, clapping Jack on the back, and as I looked at the faces around me—faces marked by sacrifice, loyalty, and a depth of understanding that only comes from shared experiences—I felt a surge of happiness for Jack.

But amidst the joy, a thread of sadness wove its way into my heart. The man I loved was going back into a life fraught with danger.

I'd be lying if I said that didn't scare me.

Jack must've sensed my emotions, because he took my hand and led me to a quiet corner of the room. "Are you okay?" he asked, his eyes searching mine for the truth.

I forced a smile. "I'm so happy that you're doing what is important to you, but I can't help but be a little scared, too. What if you get hurt? What if you don't come back?"

Jack pulled me close, his arms wrapping around me in a

comforting embrace. "I know, sweetheart. It's not easy for me either. But having you by my side makes me feel like I can face whatever comes next."

Tears welled up in my eyes as I looked up at him. "And I'll be right here, Jack, waiting for you and praying for you every step of the way."

He kissed the top of my head, holding me tight as if he could somehow fuse his strength into me. "And that, Lydie, makes all the difference."

As we stood there, enveloped in our little cocoon of love and faith, I sent up a prayer for the journey ahead.

Lord, watch over him, protect him, and bring him back to me.

Chapter Fourteen

Jack

On our way back from Jim's funeral the next day, Lydie fell asleep.

I snuck glimpses of her as I navigated the highways back to Beaufort. Her eyelashes rested on her cheeks, her lips slightly parted. She looked so peaceful as if all the burdens of the world had left her.

She was beautiful.

And, not just on the outside.

She'd always been patient with me, ready to be there when I needed her. After mom's stroke, Lydie was there, managing doctor's appointments with me, and taking late-night pharmacy runs when I couldn't leave mom by herself.

Now, with Jim's funeral, she had dropped everything to come on this trip with me.

She didn't have to, but she did— just to stand beside me and give me comfort if I needed it.

I think it was then that it happened, and I knew I would be telling this story to everyone for the rest of my life.

This was the moment I knew I was going to ask her to marry me.

Lydie had always been special to me. Her laughter filled the room like sunlight, chasing away shadows and painting everything in hues of hope.

We grew up together, our innocent friendship gradually giving way to the awkwardness of first love. She was the first girl I ever held hands with, the first girl I ever kissed.

So much of my life I experienced with her.

For over thirty years, we lived separate lives, yet in all that time, I never dated. People thought it was strange, maybe even a little sad, but they didn't understand.

I didn't want anybody that wasn't Lydie.

I buried myself in my career, in the military, even in caring for Mom, yet Lydie never left my thoughts. I'd catch myself daydreaming, imagining scenarios where we could be together.

Lydie was more than just a romantic partner; she was my confidante, my friend, my peace in a world that often felt chaotic. She stood by me always, never asking for anything in return.

She is my yesterday, my today, my forever.

She filled the empty spaces in my soul, making me a better man just by being herself. I'd loved her since I was old enough to understand what love meant, and that love had only grown from there.

I spent three decades waiting for her, missing her, loving her from a distance. Now that she's here, now that life has given me a second chance, I'm not letting her slip away. I'm going to ask Lydie to marry me.

My mind began sketching plans for a proposal.

As the car's tires hummed on the asphalt, Lydie stirred. For a second, I feared she'd wake and catch me lost in my musings. Instead, she shifted closer, her head finding the curve of her bundled-up coat serving as a makeshift pillow. A contented sigh escaped her lips.

Watching her, I thought about the road ahead—literally and metaphorically.

There would be challenges, decisions to make that would shape our future. My reenlistment loomed large among them.

As the car rolled down the highway, I locked away the uncertainty of us once I was overseas and focused instead on the proposal.

Obviously, it had to be meaningful, but where could somewhere like that exist for us?

Almost instantly, the trees in Lydie's backyard came to mind. It was that very spot underneath their canopies that I'd given her a promise ring. I could still hear our youthful voices as we made a pact to marry each other someday.

Plus, that was also where we buried the time capsule.

It had to be there. That sacred spot was not only picturesque but soaked in sentiment. It was as if those trees had stood guard over our promises, waiting patiently for us to return and fulfill them.

There, under those faithful trees, I'd drop to one knee and ask her to be my wife.

Then, my thoughts turned to the ring.

What style would she like? Would a classic diamond suit her, or should I opt for something less conventional?

Lydie was elegant in her simplicity, a woman who found beauty in the most ordinary things. Maybe a ring that captured that essence, perhaps a vintage piece with history and character, would be the perfect symbol of our enduring love.

I don't know, I'll have to do some research.

My heart started pounding just thinking about her reaction. Would she cry? Laugh?

And what would I say? The words had to encapsulate decades of love, friendship, separation, and sweet reunion. They had to speak to the future, to the unspoken dreams we still wanted to achieve, to the hurdles we'd no doubt face but conquer together.

I rehearsed lines in my head, each one sounding trite compared to the enormity of what I felt.

The miles melted away as I pondered these details, my mind painting vivid pictures of what that magic moment could be like.

As the lights of Beaufort appeared on the horizon, I felt an overwhelming sense of gratitude.

Life had given us a second chance, and this time, I was going to get it absolutely right. I had waited more than thirty years for this moment, and every choice, every word, every look would be a tribute to that love.

So, of course, the first thing I did once I was back in Beaufort was I told my mother.

"Oh my! I'm so excited!" she squealed. "I'm going to have Lydie as a daughter-in-law!"

"Well, first I need to pick out a ring, and she has to say yes."

My mom waved her hand at me like that was nothing. "She's definitely going to say yes. She is so in love with you."

I couldn't help but blush. "Do you really think so?"

She rolled her eyes. "Well, duh! Do you really think any woman would just want to hang around her boyfriend's mother all day if she didn't love and want to be with him?"

She had a point. "Yeah, I guess you're right."

"Of course, I am. So, do you know what you're going to say to her? Oh, where are you going to do it? Are you going to have someone take pictures? Oh, you should hire someone to take pictures!"

I laughed at the amount of enthusiasm my mother was giving. "Breathe, Mom, your face is turning blue. I do know where I want it to happen, but I don't know what to say. We'll take pictures later if she says yes."

"She will." My mom argued again.

"I'm really worried about the ring, though. I've been looking online, but nothing seems to suit her, you know?"

My mom scrunched her lips up in concentration. "Why don't you keep looking and then pick out your favorites? From there, you can have someone who knows Lydie help you pick."

I genuinely smiled. "Mom, you're a genius."

"I know."

As I dialed Tori's number, my palms were a bit sweaty. "Hey, Tori, it's Jack. Are you free on Tuesday? I was hoping you could come over. I've got something important I wanna talk to you about."

Then, when Tuesday rolled around, she arrived, her eyes were wide with curiosity.

"Your phone call seemed very... clandestine. I feel like I'm being pulled into a mystery novel," she said as I ushered her inside the house, little Adam hanging on her hip. "What's with the secrecy?"

I took a deep breath. "I'm gonna ask Lydie to marry me."

Tori let out a shriek of joy, making Adam jerk in her arms and give her a stern look for frightening him. "Oh my gosh, Jack, this is incredible! Aunt Lydie is gonna be so happy!"

"Yeah, I'm hoping she will be," I said, my face flushed with a mixture of happiness and relief. "There's also another reason why I called you over. I was hoping you wouldn't mind helping me pick out a ring. I want it to be really special."

Her face lit up even more. "Sure! I'll try my best."

I grinned and motioned toward the living room. She sat near my mom, perching Adam on her lap. My mom did her usual cooing at Adam, tickling his belly just the way he liked it.

I clicked the remote, and the PowerPoint slides flashed up on the TV screen. The titled slide read: What Ring To Get Lydie?

Tori burst out laughing while Mom wore a smirk. "Really, Jack? PowerPoint slides?" Mom teased.

"I wanted to be organized," I defended myself. "This is important!"

"Nobody's doubting that, honey," Mom said, still grinning. "Especially now."

Tori laughed even harder.

I decided to ignore them both and continue on.

"How many rings do you have on this presentation of yours?" Tori asked.

I frowned. "I don't know. I think, twenty. Why?"

Tori's eyes widened. "No reason. But if I'm here for more than two hours, I'm ordering a pizza."

The excitement that was buzzing through my veins deflated a bit when I saw Tori and Mom's lukewarm reactions to the slides of potential rings.

"So, what do you think?" I asked, trying to keep a hopeful tone.

Tori and Mom exchanged glances before Tori spoke, "These are lovely rings, really, but they're not... they're not Aunt Lydie."

"Yeah, son." Mom chimed in. "They're beautiful, but they don't quite scream... her, you know."

"Exactly." Tori agreed.

I sighed, letting the disappointment wash over me. "I want the ring to be as special as she is to me, you know?"

Mom reached over and patted my hand. "It's just a tricky thing, dear."

"That's true," Tori said, her eyes lighting up with a sudden idea. "You should call my mom. She would know exactly what Lydie would like. I mean, they're sisters!"

I looked at her, hopeful but slightly embarrassed. "Really? You think she'd want to help? I haven't talked to her in years."

Tori grinned. "She'd be thrilled to help."

Well, it was worth a shot. "Alright, I'll give her a call."

As soon as Mira picked up the phone and I explained why I was calling, she was audibly moved. "Oh, Jack, this is wonderful news! Of course, I'd love to help you pick a ring for Lydie."

Relief washed over me, instantly dispelling some of the disappointment from earlier. I walked Mira through what I'd researched, what Tori and Mom had said, and most importantly, what I felt in my heart Lydie would love.

Mira listened carefully before offering her insight. "Remember the pendant you got her years ago? She wore it every day until the clasp broke. She'd want something that felt both vintage and modern, a ring that tells a story."

"That's just the insight I needed," I said, grateful. "Thank you, Mira."

She chuckled softly. "Jack, I've seen the way my sister

looks at you. I've seen it for years, even when you two were apart. Helping you is my pleasure."

It took me about two days to find the perfect Honestly, I was so overwhelmed by it all that I thought about giving up — not on the proposal, of course — but I was starting to entertain ideas that involved having her pick out her own ring.

Then, I was in the checkout lane at the grocery store when I saw the necklace the cashier was wearing, and I could imagine Lydie wearing something very similar.

"I'm sorry," I started, shyly. "May I ask where you got that necklace? It's very beautiful."

Her hand went to the cross pendant before she answered. "Oh! It's my Gran's. She let me borrow it because my other one broke."

"Oh, that's lovely," I said, crestfallen.

"But," she continued, and I perked up. "I think she got this over in Greenville. There's a little antique jewelry shop there called Heaven's Blessings."

Heaven's Blessings. That couldn't be more perfect.

I thanked the clerk and rushed out the door. I didn't even stop by the house to drop off the groceries before I hit the highway. I was in Greenville in less than an hour. I followed my GPS right to the front door, and as soon as the little bell above the door rang of my arrival, I knew this was the place.

The interior smelled like old books mixed with the sweet, calming scent of lavender. Polished wooden shelves lined the walls, filled with keepsakes that ranged from vintage porcelain angels to well-loved Bibles with gold-leaf edges.

"Hello," greeted the shop owner. "My name is Esther. How can I help?"

"Oh, hi, I... I'm actually looking for a ring. I heard great things about your shop, and I wanted to know if you had any engagement rings?"

Like most everyone else I told, her eyes lit up with excitement at the news and she clapped her hands together. "Oh, I love weddings! Follow me, dear. I have a whole collection of engagement rings."

I followed her as she took me to the back of her shop, and if the front of the store hadn't already dragged me in, back here definitely would have.

Esther ushered me over to a glass display case. Inside it, a collection of divine jewelry awaited, perched on little white cushions.

Here, you'd find crosses of all sizes, some ornate with intricate engravings, others plain and simple. There were fish symbols, tiny lockets containing verses from Psalms, and even a few Jesus medals. The pieces were well-worn, each carrying its own history of faith and devotion. Some had turned a warm, burnished gold, while others held onto their original silver gleam.

Around the display case were small, handwritten tags that told a little story about each item:

"Owned by a missionary in Africa."

"Brought back from the Holy Land."

Or, "Gifted by a soldier to his wife."

I paused, immediately, staring down at the ring shining up at me.

Esther followed my line of sight. She pulled the ring from the display case and pushed it over the counter for me to look more closely.

"Oh, this is a beautiful piece," she confirmed. "I think I

got it maybe... a couple of years ago. Apparently, the story here is that a US soldier bought this ring in Germany for his wife during the Second World War for their tenth anniversary. He couldn't make it back to her in time, so he had this shipped overseas.

"This is a geometric platinum engagement ring," she explained as I plucked it from its cushion to look at it more closely. "Now, at the heart of this ring is a 0.60-carat old European cut diamond. It's got a K color and SI2 clarity. What makes it really special is the box prong setting; it keeps the diamond secure while letting it shine from all angles."

She definitely wasn't wrong about that. The more I moved the ring in the light, the more it shined. Gorgeous.

Esther held her hand out for the ring, and I dropped it into her palm. She turned the ring around and showed me the engraving on the inside that I had missed before.

"This is why it is my favorite ring."

As I looked closer, my eyes widened, even more impressed. Engraved on the inside of the band was a small cross with the words: Song of Solomon 6:3. I didn't have to reference a Bible to know the meaning of those words.

I am my beloved's and my beloved is mine.

As soon as I confirmed it would be the right size, I said, "I'll take it."

Once I had the ring, I was much more confident about the rest of my plan.

I couldn't believe this day had finally come. Thirty years of dreaming about Lydie, and today, right under the same trees where I gave her a promise ring when we were just kids, I was going to ask her to marry me.

Earlier that day, I called Tori to make sure she'd keep Lydie out of the house so I could get everything set up.

"Uncle Jack, you owe me a real good story after this," she had said, giggling.

I promised her I would.

Then, I called a neighbor and asked if they could keep an eye on my mom for most of the day. When I told them I was planning a surprise for Lydie, I'm pretty sure they knew exactly what I was referring to. I'm sure my mom was spreading the news around.

After that, I went to the florist and requested all of their rose bouquets.

"You want... *all* of the rose bouquets?" the florist asked, nervously, looking at his shelves.

I could tell that his roses were a popular item in the shop, and me leaving with all of them would leave the rest of his customers unhappy, but when I explained to him the reason behind the need, he had all members of the staff help me load up the SUV.

"I just love weddings," he beamed before handing over a different bouquet that I didn't request. When I looked at him, quizzically, he just smiled and patted my shoulder. "These are orchids. They symbolize good luck and prosperity. It's a gift from me to you and your special lady."

I was touched. "Thank you so much."

I hurried back to Lydie's place, petals carefully placed in bags and roses filling up all of the empty spaces in my car. Lydie had told me before that she kept a key under a frog in the flowerbed next to her porch, so I plucked it out and let myself in. I got to work immediately.

First things first, the trail.

Starting at the front door, I scattered rose petals, making a path that wound through the living room, snaked around the dining table, and went straight out the sliding glass door into the backyard.

Each petal felt like a breadcrumb of my love, leading her back to the best memories of us.

Next, the lighting. I opted for LED candles, safer and just as beautiful. I lined the rose-petal trail with them, imagining the soft glow that would light her way.

Finally, the spot under the two trees by the lake.

And before I did anything else, I took a deep breath and bathed in the setting sun. This was a blessed ground for us. No matter where life was leading us, we always came back to this spot. Closing my eyes, I let out a silent prayer to Our Heavenly Father above.

Lord, whatever answer Lydie gives me today, I just want her to be happy. I want her to know that no matter what, I love, cherish, and respect her. Wherever our paths may lead after tonight, I am always in Your honored embrace. Regardless of her answer, please keep shining Your guiding light on me and Lydie. Thank you, Jesus. It's in Your Mighty Name I pray. Amen.

After my prayer, I carefully arranged a circle of candles around the base of each tree, then laid down more rose petals. I planted the orchids the florist gave me in a flower pot and placed the pot in the middle of where I envisioned Lydie and I standing.

And, right on time, I heard the beep of a car door being locked and voices wafting through the breeze from the front of the house. I positioned myself where I wanted, a single rose in my hand, the box with the engagement ring in my pocket.

There, I waited.

And then I saw her.

Lit by the trail of LED candles, she looked ethereal.

Her eyes widened as she took in the rose petals, and I saw her hand go to her heart. As she walked down the trail, I felt the years, the distance, the time apart all collapse into this single, heavenly moment.

She followed the trail until she met me under the canopy of trees. I stepped out from behind the tree. Her eyes met mine and for a second, we were both seventeen again—full of dreams, love, and the promise of forever.

The moment she was in front of me, tears glistening from the corner of her eyes, I started to speak.

"Lydie, I have loved you from the moment I met you. It was my sixth birthday party, and I was the new kid in school. I didn't know anyone. I didn't have any friends, so when my mom sent out invites to my classmates, I didn't expect anyone to come. But you did. You saw the balloons outside of my house and you walked over and introduced yourself."

I smiled, remembering fondly. "You held out your hand for me to shake. You told me your name was Lydia, but you go by Lydie. You told me if I ever called you Lydia, you'd never speak to me again. It was the best birthday I ever had."

I stepped closer to her, taking her hands in mine.

"You have always been one of the most important people in my life. I have never forgotten the love I have had for you, and still do to this day. Every day, I am in awe of you. You are so caring, so thoughtful, so beautiful. I don't ever want to spend another moment without you by my side."

Then, as I went down on one knee, I let go of her hands to reach in my pocket for the box. I opened it and presented it to her.

"Please don't stop talking to me after this." I smiled at

her, tears of my own making her face blurry in my vision. "But, Lydia Marie Dawson, will you marry me?"

The tears spilled over, but her voice was unwavering. "Yes," she whispered. "A thousand times yes."

And just like that, every petal, every candle, every moment that had led us here, I was eternally grateful for.

As I kissed her, her watery, salty lips mingling with mine, I sent up another silent prayer.

Thank you, Lord, for this incredible blessing.

Chapter Fifteen

Lydie

I couldn't wipe the grin off my face as I walked through the front door, still feeling the warmth of Jack's embrace after he left that night.

He had proposed.

And, it was as if every dream and every prayer had brought us to this moment. The ring on my finger glittered in the soft light, each sparkle whispering promises of a love that defied the limits of time and distance.

That night we sat under the moonlight, already excited to plan our lives together. We'd talked, laughed, and made decisions—somehow planning a wedding in a matter of weeks felt just right. We didn't need a grand spectacle; we just needed each other, some friends and family, and the presence of God to seal our vows.

A winter wedding it would be, snowflakes and all.

But life has its own rhythms, and soon enough Jack

would be deployed. It was a conversation we'd had many times since he decided to reenlist for one final tour. It was a choice I supported, but I know as the weeks got closer and closer, he worried more and more about his mother.

"Jack," I told him that night. "When you go away for your next tour, I'd like for your mother to live with me. I can take care of her."

His eyes widened at the offer. "Really? I don't want to put that pressure on you."

I leaned in close and pressed a sweet kiss to his cheek. "Your mother is going to be my family, too, Jack. I would do anything for her."

He smiled brightly at me. "We'll talk to her tomorrow and see if she'd like that."

Honestly, when I walked over the next day, and Jack and I sat with her and explained what we had talked about, she couldn't have looked happier.

"Oh, Lydie, that sounds wonderful. Your house has the best view of the lake!" she cried out happily. "You're a godsend, truly. I couldn't ask for a better daughter-in-law."

I sat back on the couch, my hands wrapped around a warm cup of tea, and let myself soak in the enormity of it all. A wedding, a deployment—it was a whirlwind, but one that God was clearly guiding. I could feel His hand in every decision, every smile, and every tear.

Lord, I prayed silently, *thank You for this life, for the ups and downs, for the journey You're leading us on. Please watch over Jack when he's away, keep him safe, and bring him back to me and to all who love him.*

I closed my eyes and let the silence envelop me, feeling like I was wrapped in a divine embrace.

When I opened them, I was met with the comforting walls of my home, soon to be shared with a new family, in a life newly marked by the promise of everlasting love. I looked at my engagement ring one more time, its sparkle reflecting the joy and hope that filled me.

At that moment, I knew we would be alright. God was with us, and with Him, all things are possible.

Three days before the wedding, I invited Jack and Viv over for dinner.

The sun streamed through the kitchen windows as I ladled butternut squash soup into bowls. The hearty smell of the soup filled the room as I set the table. I'd been keeping a secret from Jack and Viv, and today was the day for the big reveal.

After we'd finished our meal— warm soup, a salad, and some homemade bread—Jack helped me wheel Viv's chair toward a part of the house she'd never seen, and one I had kept locked away for years.

"This is a surprise for both of you," I told them.

We rolled through the hallway, coming to the door of what used to be my parents' suite. Since they'd passed, the room had been a quiet sanctuary, sealed off and filled with memories too precious to part with.

But love, I'd found, has a way of making you see the world—and your own home—in new ways, and I wanted this space for my mother-in-law.

So, I opened the door, revealing the transformed space that took a week to perfect. Freshly painted walls, new carpeting, and carefully selected furniture filled the room.

It was beautiful, but most importantly, it was fully accessible, tailored to Viv's needs.

"Welcome to your new suite, Viv," I announced, throwing my arms out wide for her. "I left a lot of the space open for you so that you can bring over anything from your house that you wanted, but I did pick up a couple of pieces of furniture, just to brighten the place up."

I watched her eyes widen, filling with tears as she took in the renovated space.

"This is... I can't even put it into words, dear," Viv whispered, visibly moved. "I'm truly touched."

I guided her through the room, pointing out the grab bars we'd installed in the bathroom, the widened doors, and the lowered light switches. Every detail had been thoughtfully designed to make her life a little easier.

Jack came up behind me and wrapped his arms around my waist. "Lydie, this is amazing," he said softly. "Mom, you're going to love it here."

"Oh!" I jumped out of Jack's arms. "I almost forgot the best part. Here, over here."

I guided them over to the darkened space in the room. As soon as they were in place to see it in its full effect, I flipped on the light switch. I chuckled at their collective gasps.

Sheltered by natural wooden beams that arched over the ceiling, this intimate space was a beautiful escape from the world. The alcove was decorated with plush cushions and a few select throw pillows, each woven with intricate designs that told tales of homely comfort and easy Sunday mornings.

I had the walls painted in a calming hue—a soft shade, like a sleepy morning sky. Bookshelves filled with well-loved classics, and a scattering of delicate knickknacks framed the place. A small, antique table rested to one side, holding a delicately painted porcelain teapot and a pair of cups, so Viv could always be ready to entertain guests.

But the true jewel of this alcove was its panoramic

window, a generous expanse of glass. This window overlooked the lake Viv loved so much.

Through the glass, the lake lay still beneath the moonlit sky, transformed into a celestial mirror that caught the twinkle of stars and the glow of the moon above. Its surface shimmered with a silver sheen, softly rippling. Lightly, snowflakes started to fall from the sky.

"Would you look at that?" Viv sighed, staring out at the sparkling water. "It's like a little slice of heaven right here on Earth."

"I wanted this place to be as special for you as it was for my parents," I said to Viv. "I think they'd be happy knowing it's being filled with love again."

"Thank you, Lydie," Viv said, reaching out to squeeze my hand. "I cannot wait to live with you here, daughter."

Jack wrapped his arms around me, again, pulling me close, and I couldn't help but feel complete.

Sweetly, he whispered in my ear, "I love you so much, sweetheart. Thank you for taking care of us."

"Of course," I said back. "You guys are my family."

On that Saturday morning, I woke up for my wedding.

Today's the day. The sun rose, its golden rays gleaming off the dusting of snow that lightly coated the earth. A winter wedding in North Carolina.

I only had about thirty minutes of peaceful serenity before my house started filling with the sounds of people coming in and going. By the time it was nine-fifteen, I had already eaten and showered.

Now, I was sitting in a chair as my chatty hairstylist did wonders with my hair and simple makeup.

After that, Mira, my matron of honor, helped me into

my dress.

As I slipped into the gown, I couldn't help but marvel at its simple elegance. It was everything I dreamed it would be —a perfect blend of grace and understated beauty, just like the love Jack and I share.

The dress is a classic A-line silhouette, skimming the contours of my body before falling gently to the floor, like the first snow of winter. The fabric is a soft ivory, reminiscent of the aged pages of a cherished Bible. Made from a delicate blend of silk and lace, the material feels like a warm whisper against my skin. The bodice is adorned with intricate lace appliques, tiny flowers that seem to bloom right from the fabric. Modest, yet breathtaking.

The sleeves are long and sheer, a nod to the winter season, providing a hint of coverage while still letting my skin breathe. They end in delicate lace cuffs that hug my wrists.

My gown's neckline is a modest scoop, framing my collarbones in a soft, flattering curve. It's inviting but reserved, embodying the Christian values that Jack and I hold dear. The back is a tasteful V-shape, closing with a trail of petite silk buttons that Mira takes her time fastening.

About half down my back, I heard Mira groan. "You couldn't have possibly thought of going for a gown with *less* buttons."

I laughed. "You were the one who said you liked this one the most."

"Yes, but I also didn't realize I would be the one buttoning you into it. This is a lot!"

The train is my best part. It's not too long, but just enough to add a hint of drama as I walk down the aisle, and it floats behind me like a cloud.

Once Mira was done, I looked at myself in the mirror,

veiled and ready.

I can't wait to see Jack's face when he sees me.

"Mira, can you believe it? I'm getting married today," I murmured to her.

"I always knew you would find your way back to Jack," she replied, her eyes meeting mine in the mirror before gently hugging me from behind.

That afternoon, we arrived at the small, humble church where Jack and I grew up, its wooden pews and stained-glass windows familiar. The scent of pine and cinnamon permeates the air with its wintery perfume.

Simple wreaths decorated with red and white ribbons hang from the doors, and small white LED candles line the aisle, their fake flames flickering softly.

As the pianist began playing our chosen hymn, my heart leaped. Mira offered me a reassuring smile before she took my hand.

"I love you, baby sister," she whispered to me.

"I love you, big sister," I said back to her.

Together we walked down the aisle, my only other bridesmaid, Tori leading the way.

The guest list was small, but I still felt nervous walking in front of all of those people.

"Don't look at them," Mira advised me, silently. "Look at Jack."

So, I did.

Jack, standing at the altar, his eyes locking onto mine as if magnetized.

And, the world around me blurred.

It's just me, him, and the promises we're about to make before God. Suddenly, I didn't feel so anxious anymore, and by the time Mira handed Jack my hand, I had forgotten about everyone else.

Chapter Fifteen

The pastor began speaking, but Jack's gaze never wavered — as if he was silently speaking to my soul, assuring me that our love, tested and strengthened over the years, was the blessing we've both been waiting for.

"Ladies and gentlemen, if I can have your attention, please," Pastor James called attention to the congregation. "We are all gathered here today, not just to witness, but to partake in a divine moment. Marriage isn't merely a contract; it's a sacred covenant, a promise not just between two people, but between those people and God Himself.

"In the Bible, it says, 'Love is patient, love is kind.' It doesn't boast, it's not proud."

The pastor smiled at us before continuing.

"And so, when you face trials—and rest assured, trials will come—always remember that it's not just the two of you facing them. You have God on your side, and a room full of witnesses who believe in your union, who believe in the kind of love that knows no bounds."

"Now, as I've been told, Jack and Lydie have letters from their past that they would like to share with each other."

The letters from our time capsule. Mira handed me mine, and Jack pulled his out of his pocket.

Jack started reading his first, unfolding the worn pages. His eyes misted over as he quickly read the words he wrote for me all those years ago.

"'Lydie,'" he read, aloud. "'As I sit here writing this letter to you, I can't help but think of the first time we met. You were like a ray of sunshine piercing through the clouds, and I knew my life was forever changed.

"'I've heard people say that we're too young to know what true love is, that we have our whole lives ahead of us to figure it out. But I believe God places people in our lives for a reason, and when I look at you, I see the rest of my life in your eyes. I feel it in every hug, in every laugh we share, in every silent moment when words become unnecessary.'"

He took in a deep breath before continuing. "'I know life is taking us on separate paths now. You're going to college, and I've got my own journey ahead. But no amount of distance can sever what we have, Lydie. My love for you is like an unbreakable thread—no matter how far we are from each other, it will never snap, never fray.'"

Thank the heavens for waterproof mascara or I would be a mess right now.

"'So as we take these steps into the unknown, remember that I carry you in my heart, as I hope you carry me in yours. Wherever you are, look up at the sky and know that we are both under the same vast canopy of stars, stitched together by the same Creator who orchestrated our meeting.'"

Then, he finished with, "'Until we see each other again, my thoughts, my prayers, and my love will always find their way to you. You are my forever, Lydie, and that's a promise not even distance can break. With all the love in my heart, Jack.'"

"Beautiful words, Jack," Pastor James complimented. "Lydie, are you ready?"

"Yes, Pastor."

"'Dear Jack,'" I started, staring down at the words I had written when I was just on the bridge of adulthood. "'As I sit down to write this letter, I can't help but feel amazed by how life has a way of bringing two souls together, intertwining them in ways neither could have anticipated. I thank God every day for the blessing that is you—for your laughter, your wisdom, and the genuine kindness that radiates from your soul.'"

From the pews, I heard a few "awws". It gave me the

confidence to continue on.

"'We're still so young, yet it feels like we've known each other a lifetime. Your presence in my life has been like a steady lighthouse, always guiding me back to what's important—love, family, and God's grace.

"'I don't know what the future holds, but I do know this —I will always love you, Jack. You have a special place in my heart, one that time or distance can never erase. Whatever paths we take, wherever we end up, my prayers will always be with you. I pray for your happiness, your success, and most importantly, for God's love to always envelope you.

"'We are both embarking on separate journeys, yet I can't shake the feeling that our stories are far from over. I am hopeful, as always, that our paths will cross again under God's perfect timing. Until then, take this letter as a small token of my love and gratitude. Know that you are cherished, not just by me, but by everyone lucky enough to know you. You are destined for great things, Jack Lawrence. I can't wait to see the incredible man you will become. With all my love and prayers, Lydie.'"

After finishing the letter, and handing it back to my sister, Jack whispered the words only I could hear, "I love you."

I giggled. "I love you, too."

Pastor James looked at Jack. "Do you have the rings?"

Jack smiled, happily. "Yes, I do."

The room filled with a quiet energy of reverence, as everyone prepared their hearts for the solemn vows about to be spoken.

Pastor James asked, "Lydie, Jack, are you ready to make this beautiful promise under God?"

We both nodded.

"Jack, will you please repeat after me?"

"Certainly, Pastor."

"I, Jack, take you, Lydie, to be my lawfully wedded wife. To have and to hold, from this day forward."

Jack repeated the words.

Pastor James then said, "For better, for worse; for richer, for poorer; in sickness and in health."

Again, Jack repeated the words.

"To love and to cherish, as long as we both shall live, under God's grace."

Jack stated, "To love and to cherish, as long as we both shall live, under God's grace."

Pastor James said, "Lydie, your turn to make this sacred promise. Please repeat after me."

Lydie replied, "Of course, Pastor."

After we finished the vows, said our "I dos", Pastor James pronounced us husband and wife.

"Jack, you may now kiss your wife."

And there, before the eyes of God and the people we loved the most, Jack leaned forward and kissed me.

After the ceremony, we made our way to the modest reception area that had been set up in the church's fellowship hall. Tables were dressed in white and gold, centerpieces of holly and pine cones artfully arranged.

Jack and I shared our first dance to a classic love song that filled the room. As I laid my head on his shoulder, my thoughts drifted to our future. I imagined us old and gray, sitting in our cozy alcove, overlooking a serene lake, thanking God every day for this gift.

Two days after our wedding day, Jack and I boarded the plane to Paris. We said our goodbyes to our family, appeased by the fact that Viv would be staying with Tori and her family while we were away.

I was fine up until the turbulence started rocking the cabin. I gasped in fear, my hand flying out to find Jack's hand. He intertwined his fingers with mine.

"Oh, are you scared, love?" Jack asked.

"I'm just..." I gulped. "I... don't like flying."

Jack removed his hand from mine so that he could reach across the seats and put his arm over my shoulder, drawing me into the safety of his embrace. I tucked my head into his neck and closed my eyes.

"It's okay," he assured me. "It'll be over in a few moments."

I could only groan in response.

"Also," he continued. "Did you know that more deaths are caused by vehicles than in a plane crash? Does that make you feel better?"

"No," I whined. "Now, I'm afraid of cars, too."

Through his shirt, I could feel the laughter rumbling in his chest.

"I'm sorry, my love. Try to take your mind off of it. That should help."

"How?"

"Just think of something happy."

"Like what?"

I felt his lips go to my ear as he whispered only for me to hear. "Well, I certainly like to think of our wedding night for one."

I gasped, blushing and slapping his belly playfully. "Jack Lawrence Weston, don't be crude!"

He just laughed harder. "I can't help it, Mrs. Weston. I just love you so much."

Of course, I smiled. "I love you, too, Mr. Weston."

Hours later, the plane landed with a gentle thud, and my heart skipped a beat.

"We're here, Lydie," Jack whispered, his voice tinged with excitement. He took my hand, squeezing it as if to assure himself this was real.

After we left the Charles de Gaulle airport, we made our way through the charming cobblestone streets, our breaths visible in the crisp winter air.

Paris in winter is a dream.

The City of Love is quieter in winter, wrapped in a blanket of soft snow and mist.

Jack hailed a taxi, and we were soon on our way to the little hotel we had booked, nestled in the heart of Montmartre. The driver weaved through narrow lanes, past cafes where people sipped steaming cups of hot chocolate and coffee, bundled up in coats and scarves. It was magical, like a scene from a painting.

We checked in, and the concierge, a petite woman with a warm smile, led us to our room. Jack opened the door, and I gasped. It's beautiful—simple, with a vintage charm. But what caught my eye was the window—the large, almost floor-to-ceiling window that offered a panoramic view of the city, the Sacré-Cœur Basilica standing majestically in the distance.

After the concierge left, and the door closed behind her, Jack pulled me into his arms as we gazed out the window.

"We have the most beautiful view," he said.

"We do," I agreed, snuggling into his arms. We stood there for a few moments, taking it all in—the view, the warmth, the overwhelming sense of love that fills the room.

Over the course of the next few days, we explored the city.

We walked hand-in-hand down the Seine River, its

waters reflecting the soft gray of the winter sky. Street musicians filled the air with melodies, their notes dancing like snowflakes around us. We crossed bridges crowded with love locks, the names of couples etched onto them, immortalizing their love.

At one point, Jack took me to a little café he read about.

"Le Coeur de Paris," he said, his accent endearing.

We ordered a simple meal—warm, crusty bread, creamy cheese, and a pot of steaming tea. As we dined, Jack reached over the table to hold my hand. "I love you, Lydie, more than anything in this world. God has blessed me immensely by bringing you into my life."

My eyes welled with tears. "I love you, too, Jack. I still can't believe we're here, together."

He grinned. "Believe it, sweetheart. You make every moment, every place, a dream come true."

We wrapped up our meal and made our way back to the hotel. The streets were quieter now, the snow beginning to fall in earnest.

Back in our room, we curled up under the warm blanket, the city lights twinkling through our window. Jack held me close, and I rested my head on his chest, listening to the steady rhythm of his heart.

"I prayed for this, you know," I whispered. "For a love like ours. For moments like this."

Jack kisses the top of my head. "God answers prayers, Lydie. He gave me you, and that's the greatest answer to prayer I've ever received."

As I closed my eyes, grateful beyond words, I realized this was just the beginning. Our honeymoon in Paris was the start of a lifetime filled with love, and God-willing, countless more winters to come.

Chapter Sixteen

Jack

Dusty air and the harsh sun painted the backdrop of my days here in Iraq.

We were far from Beaufort, from the cool breeze by the lake and the soft rustle of leaves in those trees where I promised Lydie forever. But even amid the noise of armored vehicles and the sporadic gunfire, I carried that piece of home in my heart.

Serving there, it's like walking on a tightrope every day. One misstep, one wrong decision, and things can go sideways fast. My platoon counts on me, and every time I put on that uniform, I think about them—the eager faces wanting to serve, but also wanting nothing more than to go back to their loved ones.

Just like me.

I keep a photo of Lydie tucked into the pocket of my uniform, close to my heart. When things get rough, I take a quiet moment to look at it, drawing strength from her smile. Leaving her and my mother to serve another tour was the hardest decision I've ever made. Yet, I felt it was something I had to do, especially after losing Jim. It was a way to honor him and to find some sort of closure for myself and the rest of the guys.

I video-call Lydie whenever I can, savoring the sight and sound of her. The way her eyes light up when she sees me, it's the balm for my weary soul.

"Hello, my lovely soldier!" she would say each time.

"Hello, my beautiful wife," I would greet her back.

Every day, I pray for the strength to make it through this, for the safety of my men, and most of all, for a future where the only skies I wake up to are the ones over Beaufort, next to Lydie.

The chaplain here often reminds us that faith can move mountains, and as I bow my head and send up a prayer, I hold onto the hope that it can certainly carry one soldier back to the love of his life.

So I keep going, holding onto the promise of "us," counting the days till I can exchange this desert for the welcoming arms of the woman I love. Till then, I find comfort in the Bible, in letters from home, in the camaraderie of my platoon, and in the unwavering belief that love can withstand even the harshest of deserts.

Sixteen months, I waited, and then finally I was able to go home.

As the plane touched down on American soil, my heart felt like it was doing cartwheels in my chest. Months of patrolling foreign landscapes, of tense moments and sleepless nights—they were all behind me now. I'd made it. A feeling of relief washed over me so potent it felt like I'd been holding my breath for the entire tour.

As we disembarked and made our way through the terminal, I thought of Lydie and Mom. I'd played this moment in my mind a thousand times, imagining their faces, the joy and relief we'd all feel. But imagination paled in comparison to the real thing, and as I turned a corner, there they were.

Mom looked radiant, her eyes shining with tears of happiness. And Lydie—she was a vision, standing next to Mom like an angel who had walked straight out of one of my dreams. Time seemed to slow as I rushed toward them, my duffel bag suddenly weightless, my fatigue forgotten.

Lydie's eyes met mine, and for a second, nothing else mattered. We were in our own world, our own little bubble of happiness. And then, I was holding her, feeling her arms around me, and it was as if I'd found a missing piece of my soul. Her scent filled my senses, grounding me in a way nothing else could.

"Welcome home, soldier," she whispered, her voice tinged with emotion.

Mom was next, and as I hugged her, I felt the years, the worries, the distance just melt away.

"I've prayed every day for your safe return," Mom said, holding me tight.

"Your prayers worked, Mom," I replied, my own eyes misty. "I'm here, I'm home, and it's all because of you two."

"Don't thank us too much just yet," Lydie warned. "We have more surprises in store for you."

As we reached home and I stepped out of the car, the fresh Beaufort air filling my lungs, I felt a profound sense of peace envelop me.

As Lydie pulled into the driveway, I felt a thrill of anticipation. We were back in Beaufort, the place that had always felt like home to me, and I couldn't wait to see what life had in store for us.

But what I wasn't expecting was the burst of laughter and chatter that greeted us as Lydie opened the front door.

"Surprise! Welcome home, Jack!"

I was stunned. The living room was packed with familiar faces—all smiles and eyes glistening with emotion. My eyes met Lydie's, and she gave me a wink.

"I hope you're hungry," she whispered, pulling me further into the room.

I couldn't believe it—she had prepared a feast. The aroma of home-cooked food filled the air, a tantalizing mix of roast chicken, fresh-baked bread, and some kind of pie that made my mouth water just smelling it

I felt a hand on my shoulder and turned to find Tori, grinning up at me.

"Welcome back, Uncle Jack," she said, hugging me tightly. "We missed you."

One by one, neighbors and friends came up to me, shaking my hand, slapping me on the back, each expressing their gratitude for my service. I was touched, overwhelmed even, by the outpouring of love and respect. This was my community, my home, and the feeling of being cherished by the people who mattered most was almost too much to bear.

As the evening progressed, I was swept into conversations, catching up on all the news and events I'd missed. Everyone seemed genuinely interested in hearing my stories.

Yet amid all the joy, my eyes kept drifting back to Lydie. She was the life of the party, her laughter ringing out, her face glowing with happiness. Yet, every once in a while, she'd catch my eye and give me a smile that was meant just for me.

As the night wound down and people started to leave, I found myself standing under the trees out by the lake, next to Lydie.

"Did you enjoy your surprise?" she asked.

"It was perfect," I said, kissing her once, twice, three times on the cheek. "But the best part is being right here, with you."

She looked up at me, her eyes filled with a love so deep it took my breath away.

"Welcome home, Jack," she said softly.

The sun was setting over the lake, painting the sky in shades of gold and amber. I wrapped my arms around her, breathing in the sweet scent of her hair, a mix of vanilla and summer evenings.

"Do you remember when we were just kids, Lydie? I gave you that promise ring right here," I said.

She smiled, her eyes lighting up as if she was revisiting that tender moment in her mind. "How could I forget? We were so young, so full of dreams."

"And here we are, living those dreams," I added.

In the years since that day, life took us down many winding paths. There were obstacles and heartaches, but we found our way back to each other, back to this place.

Her smile widened, and she reached up to place a gentle hand on my cheek. "I love you, Jack. You're my forever and always."

The words hit me like a tidal wave, filling my heart until it felt like it could burst. "I love you, too, Lydie. More than words can say."

We stood there for a moment, lost in each other, until she spoke up again. "Do you want to pray?"

Chapter Sixteen 177

"Yes," I said, taking her hands in mine as we both closed our eyes.

"Dear Heavenly Father," she began, her voice tinged with emotion, "thank You for bringing us back to each other, for making all things work together for Your good."

"Thank You for this place," I continued, "for these trees, this lake, and the memories that bind us to them."

Lydie's grip tightened on my hands. "Please guide us in the days to come. Help us to love each other more deeply, to support each other more fully."

"And most of all," I added, "help us to always keep You at the center of our relationship, guiding us in all that we do. In Jesus' Name we pray, Amen"

"Amen," we said in unison, opening our eyes and looking at each other as if seeing each other for the first time.

And maybe, in a way, we were. Because no matter how many times I looked into those eyes, I found something new to love, something new to cherish.

"You know, they say when you pray together, you stay together," Lydie said softly.

"I believe that," I replied. "In fact, I count on it."

She laid her head against my chest, listening to the steady beat of my heart, a rhythm that I swore only played for her.

"Here's to forever, Lydie," I said, holding her close, my eyes misty but my vision clearer than it had ever been.

She looked up at me, her own eyes shining with tears of joy. "To forever, Jack."

As we stood there, beneath the trees that have stood sentinel over so many pivotal moments in our lives, I couldn't help but feel that this was just the beginning. A new chapter in a love story that I prayed would have no end. Because with Lydie by my side, and the Lord guiding our steps, I knew we were headed for a happily ever after.

And as I held her, in this small town, surrounded by the people I loved, I knew that I was finally, truly home.

Epilogue

Lydie

Sixteen months, Viv and I waited for Jack to return to us.

Sixteen long months, a collection of days woven with anticipation and holding on to hope. Every day, I woke up, wishing and praying for Jack's safe return.

The bakery became my sanctuary, my refuge in this waiting season. My hands found comfort in the familiarity of kneading dough and icing cupcakes. Each morning, as the golden hues of dawn kissed the world awake, I would step into that warm space and get to work, breathing in the scent of baking bread and fresh coffee. It was in this place that I found the strength to forge on, even in Jack's absence.

As word spread and more customers from other states ventured into *Southern Sweets and Pies*, I knew it was time to expand, to embrace the growth, and build a future we could both be proud of. So, while Jack was away, I renovated a new space, one much bigger to house all of my culinary needs. The new space was a labor of love, brimming with natural light and infused with homely warmth.

As the bakery grew, so did the need for more staff. Every hand that joined my team became a part of a family. Among the new recruits was a gifted pastry chef, a young woman with a fire in her heart and a gift for creating mouthwatering desserts that rivaled my own.

Yet, even amidst the hustle and bustle, my heart ached for Jack. I clung to his letters and his phone calls, his words a balm to my soul, soothing the edges of my loneliness and fear.

Viv became more than just my mother-in-law during this period; she became my rock, my confidant. We spent countless hours together, sharing stories, and reminiscing about the beautiful moments she shared with her son. It wasn't always easy. There were days when worry clawed at my heart, the "what-ifs" circling like a relentless storm. But Viv reminded me to trust, to lean on our faith and to believe in the promises we'd made to each other.

If I wasn't at the bakery, Viv and I often found ourselves gravitating toward Tori's home.

Adam, a swirling vortex of energy and wonder, had blossomed into a rambunctious four-year-old. His laughter was a delightful sound that danced through the air, filling spaces with light and invoking smiles wherever it landed.

Oh, how I loved that little boy, with his inquisitive nature and boundless spirit.

Plus, seeing Adam with Viv was the sweetest thing. Their bond was special, a precious bridge between generations, built with tender moments and nurturing affection. It was as if they spoke a secret language that no one else could understand.

Epilogue 181

Tori was my closest friend in these trying times, carrying the aura of strength and maternal grace as her body nurtured another precious life. The air vibrated with anticipation, pulsating with the sweet magic that preceded the arrival of a new baby. She and I spent afternoons folding tiny clothes and arranging a new welcoming nursery, enjoying the quiet moments of a shared familial bond.

Then, as if the day would never come, Jack was back, and he was in my arms.

That night, after his welcome party had wound down, and we stood together under the trees that had been such a pivotal part of our love story, I knew without a doubt that God had graced us both with His heavenly light.

Beneath these very trees, Jack's hand enveloped mine — the familiar weight of our intertwined fingers grounding me in memories that spanned both time and emotion. The leaves above us rustled in the wind and whispered tales of our past.

Our journey began innocently, just two young souls navigating the fragility of first love. I could still recall the heady rush of emotions, the tremble in our voices when we had exchanged those three little words for the first time. We were just seventeen then, the world seemed so vast, and love so limitless. The promise ring Jack gifted me under this canopy all those years ago was a pledge, not just of love, but of dreams we hoped to fulfill.

The heartache of separation at eighteen felt like a chasm too vast to bridge. And yet, deep down, the embers of our love continued to glow, refusing to be extinguished. The time capsule we buried together here, under our feet, became a silent keeper of our hopes, dreams, and promises — one such promise that we would find our way back here.

Decades rolled by without each other. There were

moments of sheer joy, profound sadness, pain, and loneliness. The world outside changed, but our hearts remained the same, waiting patiently for us to return them to one another.

And return, we did.

Standing here now, I am reminded of how beautiful our love story really is, with all its intricacies, challenges, and rekindled passions. We've been each other's compass, pulling and guiding back to one another, no matter the distance or the passage of time. Ours wasn't just a tale of young love, but one of rediscovery, of finding one's soulmate not just once, but twice in a lifetime.

Jack's fingers squeezed mine gently, bringing me back to the present. In his gaze, I saw the reflection of our past, the clarity of our present, and the hope for our future.

A gust of wind danced through the trees, ruffling our hair and making the leaves above us flutter and sing. It was as if nature itself was celebrating our love.

With Jack by my side, I realized that love wasn't just about the big moments, the grand gestures, or the dramatic turns. It was about the small, quiet moments; the shared glances and the comforting silences.

As the golden light of the setting sun filtered through the trees, casting a luminous glow all around, I whispered a silent prayer of gratitude. For in this lifetime, amidst the vast tapestry of existence, I had been blessed with a love story that was, in every sense of the word, beautifully infinite.

About the Author

K. C. Kirkland is an emerging author/publisher of clean romance. She lives in Texas with her two fur babies, and she enjoys creating books that bring joy.

To join K.C. Kirkland's Newsletter and get a free book, click the link below.

https://dl.bookfunnel.com/hxrgsuuvgn

Follow K.C. Kirkland's author page on Amazon. Note: There are two K.C. Kirklands on Amazon. The Links provided in this book lead to the correct Author page for future books from K.C. Kirkland from Texas.

http://amazon.com/author/kckirklandtexas

Direct link to a previous book- *Tori and her Billionaire Grump*

My Book

Made in the USA
Las Vegas, NV
29 January 2025